GLASGOW FAIRYTALE

GLASGOW FAIRYTALE

ALASTAIR D. McIVER

BLACK & WHITE PUBLISHING

First published 2010
by Black & White Publishing Ltd
29 Ocean Drive, Edinburgh EH6 6JL

1 3 5 7 9 10 8 6 4 2   10 11 12 13

ISBN: 978 1 84502 330 0

A CIP catalogue record for this book is available from the British Library.

Typeset by Ellipsis Books Limited Glasgow

Printed and bound by MPG Books Ltd, Bodmin

ACKNOWLEDGEMENTS

Without author, storyteller and all-round wonderful person Lari Don, this book would exist, but it would be a very different shape. And not as good. She's a wise, wise woman!

Gale Winskill believed in the book from the start, a long time ago. And became involved once again, proving that it is, indeed a funny old world! Thank you.

The storytellers of Scotland, especially Glasgow, need a mention. Without you guys, the magic beans from which this book sprouted would never have been planted in my mind.

All at Unity also earned my thanks by giving me an insight, over the years, into what life is really like for asylum seekers. They're also a seriously good bunch of people.

And the following people who have believed in me over the years: Mrs Holmes, Miss O'Donnell, Colin McAllister, Sheena McGinnis and my wonderful family, especially Dame Doddlipoos of the Truncatit Hooses o' Wonderland.

Oh, dear. I almost forgot Jacob and Wilhelm Grimm, Charles Perrault and Hans Christian Andersen, whose fault it is that I even know any fairytales!

And last, but not least, my thanks to the varied and wonderful people of Glasgow, without whom this would all be a bit pointless.

For Florence and Precious.
May you live happily ever after in Glasgow.

CHAPTER 1

Once upon a time in Glasgow, Jack Cameron made a wish; a wish that would not come true.

He wished with all his heart that the wee drunk man who had just boarded the bus would sit next to someone else.

The man's clothes were manky, his yellowish beard (that might have been white if clean) almost trailed along the ground, and he moved with the unmistakable gait of the Glasgow drunkard. Even when the bus was still, he walked as if on the deck of a ship in a storm.

After the bus driver had explained to him three times that he was showing the back of his ticket, he stumbled up the aisle towards the very seat Jack occupied, and sat not beside, but *on* Jack.

'Sorry about that, mate,' he said, without pronouncing any consonants. He reeked of alcohol and body odour.

Jack groaned inwardly.

'Y'awright?' said the wee man.

'Awright?' said Jack, wishing the man would go away.

'Where ye off to?' said the man.

'I'm off to visit my sister,' Jack replied with an air of resignation.

'Yer sister, aye?' said the wee man, nodding and chewing, digesting this information. 'Yer sister, aye,' he trailed off, muttering the word 'sister' over and over for a minute or so, before looking up suddenly. 'What's yer sister's name?'

'Jill.'

'Jill?' said the wee man, his eyes glazed over in a moment of deep intro-spection. 'Naw, don't think I know her. Where's she stay?'

Jack cleared his throat, and said, 'Some weather we've been getting, eh?' not eager to discuss his sister's home address.

'Aye, weather, aye,' slurred the man. 'Oh, aye, it's some weather . . . aye, weather . . . aye.'

He sat in silence for a few moments, before giving Jack an almighty nudge. 'I'm no bothering ye or that?'

'No,' said Jack.

'Ye sure?'

'Aye.'

'Sure I'm no bothering ye?'

'Aye.'

Jack decided to ignore him.

Suddenly, the man sang at the top of his lungs:

> Harry Charming!
> Harry Charming!
> Harry Charming is the king of kings!

Then he gave Jack what he clearly thought was a friendly shove.

'Ye support the Celtic, big man?'

Jack shook his head, forcefully wishing that this ordeal would end.

The wee man roared with laughter and gave him another shove. 'You're alright mate.' Then, pronouncing each syllable separately (but still not pronouncing any consonants) 'You – are – all – right!'

Jack smiled and nodded.

'I'm no a bigot,' said the man, pointing at Jack for emphasis, his finger wandering aimlessly. 'I'm no a bigot,' he repeated. Then, pointing even more sternly, 'I am *not* a bigot. No way.' He poked Jack in the face. 'Makes nae difference to me if ye're a Celtic supporter or a Hun!'

Another moment's silence passed, then the wee man said, 'Buy some magic beans!' Just like that. A command.

Jack put his hands up in front of him and said firmly, 'Naw. I'm no into that, mate.'

The wee man laughed. 'Och, no. No, I'm no trying to sell ye anything bad or that. Here . . .' He fumbled in his pocket and brought out what appeared to be a handful of glowing, electric-blue marbles.

Jack was strangely transfixed. They seemed to shimmer with energy and he could almost swear he heard them humming faintly.

'See, ye plant these in the ground, like seeds or that, see. Just like seeds. Ye plant them in the ground. See the ground? Just like they was seeds, ye plant them. And out of the ground will grow your fortune!' With the word 'fortune', the wee man threw his arms wide to illustrate the magnificence of the word.

'Uh huh,' said Jack, trying not to look sceptical.

The wee man started trying to force them into his hand. 'Go on. Take them. Only two quid!'

Jack resisted.

Suddenly, in no way Jack could definitely measure, the wee man's face changed: absolutely sober he looked Jack straight in the eye with an ice-cold gaze that would have cut glass.

'Take them,' said the wee man, with perfect clarity and an air of authority far removed from the drunkard he appeared to be. 'It's your destiny.'

Jack gulped and stuffed the beans into his pocket.

'That's two pounds I'm wanting for that,' said the wee man, once again the pathetic drunkard.

'I'm no paying two pounds for a haundfu' o' jauries!' Jack exclaimed, outraged.

'You's trying to steal my magic beans!' slurred the enraged drunk. 'Haw, everybody,' he roared for all to hear. 'He's trying to steal my magic beans! Haw, driver! Get the polis! He's trying to steal my magic beans!'

'I've only got £1.75,' said Jack, fumbling in his pocket, caring more about silencing the embarrassing wee man than anything else.

'Sold.' The man took his money and promptly left the bus.

'He seen you coming, mate,' said the man sitting behind Jack.

Jack blushed as he heard clearly whispered remarks such as 'Magic beans? That's a new wan', 'That's a wee shame for that guy', 'Imagine paying two quid for that', and 'That guy's a pure numpty, by the way'.

Jack stared at his purchase: five luminous marbles. He was so angry – with himself, with the wee man, with the marbles, and with everyone on the bus who had dared to see him humiliated – that he stood up on the seat and slung the magic beans out the window.

As chance would have it, the bus was on its way over the Squinty Bridge at the time. The magic beans cleared the railing and landed, with five tiny splashes, in the River Clyde below.

Every day, after a hard workout at the gym, TV heart-throb Reginald King would uncover his own special mirror and say, 'Who's the bonniest man in Glesga then?'

And a horrible, twisted, gruesome, green face would appear in the mirror and say, 'Why, you are, Mr King.'

It was true. By most standards, Reginald King was the most handsome man in Glasgow. He had a smooth face, twinkling blue eyes and a muscle-bound body, but was so vain that no one liked him very much. They pretended to like him, for he was rich and powerful, but behind his back they said awful, dreadful things.

King never gave a hoot! He was so in love with himself that he scarcely even noticed when his girlfriend left him.

Meanwhile, Jill Cameron (aforementioned ex-girlfriend of Mr King) was busily chucking his stuff out the window.

She heard a key turning in the lock and knew it must be her brother, Jack. She continued assisting the absent Reginald with his flitting.

'Jill? Jill what are ye doing?'

'Tossing the weasel's personal effects oot the windae,' she replied calmly, and continued to do so.

'Och, don't be an eejit, Jill . . .' Jack's pierced eyebrows knitted together under his bleached hairline. 'Jill, this is crazy! We're twenty floors up! You could hurt somebody! Jill!'

Jill paid him no heed and began unplugging King's computer.

'Come on, Jill! Ye cannae fling PCs oot a twenty-storey flat!'

Jill hesitated. 'It's a Mac,' she informed him, and out it went.

Jack swore and dashed to the window. 'Oh, my God, Jill . . . I think you've killed somebody!'

'What? No!'

Jill turned pale and threw herself at the window.

'Made ye look,' said Jack.

Jill went red with fury. 'That's not funny!'

'Wasnae meant to be,' Jack explained. 'What would ye do if that had hit a wean? Going to jail would be the easy part. You'd never forgive yersel'.'

For a moment Jill flared up with rage at Jack's cruel trick, but it quickly passed as she realised he had a point. She slid to the floor, defeated, grabbing at handfuls of her hair.

'I take it you've broke into that cairry-oot wi'oot me, then?'

'Maybe . . .'

'What happened?' asked Jack.

'I'm fed up wi' him. Fed up wi' being treated like dirt. Fed up wi' him thinking he's God's gift to women. Fed up wi' women agreeing.

'You know what he says to me? He says, "You're lucky to have someone like me. Someone who'll stick with ye no matter what ye look like. There's hunners o' women would give their right arms to be wi' me."'

'Well they're welcome to him! I've had enough!'

'Good for you,' said Jack. 'You're too good for him.'

'He's right, though,' sniffled Jill. 'I mean, look at me. I'm short and fat and naebody else would want me.'

'That's not true,' insisted Jack.

She threw him an old newspaper. The front-page headline read: TV LEGEND KING DATES SHORT, FAT BURD.

'Och, ye don't want to be listening to what newspapers say! You're gorgeous, and there'll be a guy who sees that. Someday your prince will come, I guarantee it. Haud on, I'll grab us some coffees.'

By the time Jack had returned with the steaming cups, Jill had calmed down a bit.

'Anyway,' she said, 'I think we've talked quite enough about my love life. How about yours? How's Rapunzel?'

Jack broke into a huge grin.

'Given that you're still grinning like a Cheshire cat every time I mention her, I'd guess pretty well, right?'

'Och, I cannae help it. She's lovely! I love her hair. You'd never know by looking at her how long it is when she lets it doon. And she smells like apples.'

Jill chuckled. 'Glad somebody's happy. Does Maw know you're going out wi' an asylum seeker?'

Jack's grin vanished. 'Um . . . I was waiting for the right moment to mention it.'

'Well, good luck wi' that,' said Jill.

Jack gulped.

'Still, it could've been worse,' said Jill. 'She could've been a Catholic.'

Late at night, the lights were off throughout the building, except for one dim lamp in a windowless room.

A man in a suit leaned dangerously across the desk at the councillor behind it.

'What are you saying to me? I understood you had enough clout with the Planning Department to see our application through without a hitch. My client's flung a lot of money at you. Now can you deliver, or can't you?'

'There's been an unexpected complication . . . completely out of my hands,' said the councillor, trembling slightly.

'What sort of complication?'

'There's a pig. He's built a house right in the middle of your proposed development site.'

'How much does he want for it?'

'You know pigs can't be bought. This little pig built his dream home with his own trotters, out of straw, and he's well proud of it.'

'That's ridiculous! We've worked hard for this, put in a lot of dosh, bent a lot of rules and twisted more than a couple of arms. We are not going to be stopped by a grumphie!'

'Hmm,' said the councillor. 'I understand how you feel. Since animals with the power of speech were granted human rights by the European Union, they've been popping up everywhere, making a nuisance of themselves. And *they* don't need to apply for planning permission!'

'Fix this!' said the developer. 'You made a promise and unexpected complication or no, we *own* you!'

'I'm sorry, but it's out of my hands,' said the councillor. 'My question to you is how badly do you want these flats built on this particular site?'

'What do you suggest?'

'Persuasion,' said the councillor. He scribbled down a number on a yellow Post-it note and handed it to the other man. 'This guy'll sort ye out, no problem. They call him the Wolf. Probably because . . . he's a wolf.'

'An animal? Can he be trusted?'

'If the price is right, implicitly. You didnae get that from me, mind.'

'Didnae get what from you?' asked the developer, pocketing the piece of paper.

Diary of Ella McCinder

What a nightmare my life is! I hate it here!

I keep telling them I'm sixteen, well capable of looking after myself, but because I'm on this supervision thingy, that doesn't count for much.

So unfair!

The people I'm living with are just horrible. They've got two daughters who are older than me, and they're so ugly but they think they're so beautiful, and they're always telling me to do things like scrub the floor and clean the toilet and bathe all seven of their horrible dogs and - get this - clean under their toenails! And their mum and dad let them away with it!

The worst thing is they say if I tell the social workers what's going on, they'll make sure I get sent somewhere even worse and never see Mum again. I don't know if I should believe them or not, but I do know I have to hide this diary.

The only thing I'm really living for at the moment is Harry Charmaine. He's going to be interviewed by Reggie King next week, and I'm doing Work Experience at the studio, so there's a chance, just a chance, I might actually get to meet him!

I know this sounds stupid, but I love him. I really do.

Another great day in the office was followed by yet another great workout in the gym. Reginald King was very happy when he asked his mirror: 'Awright, Mirror?'

'Awright, Mr King?' replied the horrible visage that appeared in the glass.

'Who's the bonniest man in Glesga, then?' asked King, stroking his own hair.

For the first time, the mirror hesitated. 'You know, Mr King, that I can only give you an honest answer . . . but you're no gonnae like it.'

King's eyes narrowed. He looked at the mirror sideways and picked up a dumbbell. 'What are you saying to me, Mirror? Who's the bonniest man in Glesga?'

'I beg you, Mr King, not to do anything rash wi' that dumbbell. There is a young man by the name of Karl White, a strapping young lad from the Highlands, who has made this city his home. He's an albino, and everybody cries him "Snowy" on account of his white hair. His skin is softer, his smile is warmer, his eyes shine brighter, and by every measure, it must be said . . . he is bonnier than you.'

It had never occurred to Reginald King that the question he asked every day might, one day, have a different answer. His brain just wasn't wired to deal with that.

A wave of unbearable heat swept through his body; he felt a loss of control, and his fist tightened around the dumbbell until it hurt. King's heart was a ball of rage, and his voice, when it spat, *'What?'* was entirely unfamiliar to him, as if some demon had spoken in his stead.

'Try to calm down, Mr King,' said the mirror.

'Calm down?' demanded King. 'I'll do nae such thing! How dare you? Who do you think you are? You're just a wee daud o' glass, a swing o' this dumbbell away fae never insulting me again!'

He held the dumbbell over his head, ready to strike.

'You know I can neither insult nor flatter, only tell the truth. And if you smash me, you lose your only channel to the truth. There'll still be another man in Glesga bonnier than you. And others, bonnier still, may join him, but you'll never know. So go ahead, smash me. Live yer life in torment, as other men do, never knowing who's bonnier than them and who isnae.'

'What do you suggest?' puffed King, still gripping the dumbbell.

'Well, I'm loathe to go Lady Macbeth, but . . . have you considered that maybe your anger is a wee bit misdirected? If White were to have a wee *accident*, you'd never have to worry about being second bonniest again . . . well, until next time.'

'Can I do it? Can I take a human life? No! It's unthinkable!'

'Ye've nae qualms aboot doing in an innocent mirror!' spat the mirror. 'You're a racist, that's what you are! In any event, I'm no suggesting you dae yer ain dirty work.'

'Who else would?'

'What about that work experience girl, McCinder?'

King shrugged. 'Barely exchanged two words wi' her. She's nice enough . . . certainly doesnae seem the murdering type.'

'Aye,' said the mirror, 'and you can aye tell the "murdering type" by their protruding brows, close-set eyes and heavy metal tattoos.'

'Point taken,' grunted King, stung by the mirror's sarcasm.

'The girl is precisely what you're looking for. She's confused, partly because she's a teenager, and partly because her life has been turned upside down; her maw's in jail, so she's been taken into care, and her foster family are giving her a right hard time.

'She picked your studio for work experience because she's infatuated with that footballer Harry Charmaine, who you're interviewing next week.'

King seemed startled. 'I thought she was infatuated wi' me.'

'She's attracted to his kindness and warmth.'

'Ach, well,' shrugged King. 'She's young.'

'Also, when was the last time you scored against England?'

'A very good point,' conceded King, smiling. It was important to him to know that if a lady fancied another man more, it wasn't on account of his looks.

'The point is she's confused, vulnerable and desperate. That makes her easy to manipulate. Talk to her. Be her friend. Tell her you have contacts in the judiciary who could get her mum released early. Tell her you can make all her dreams come true with Charmaine. Tell her you have contacts in the Social Work Department who could make her life even worse. Then, when she's been carroted and sticked into submission, tell her to cut White's heart out and bring it to you!'

'That's revolting! Why do I have to ask for his heart?'

The mirror drew a deep, exasperated breath. 'Because, you glaikit-looking dunderheid, even once you have her cooperation, she's bound to do less than you ask. Tell her to hurt him, she'll scare him. Tell her to kill him, she'll hurt him. If you want her to *kill* him, you must tell her to mutilate him.'

Dumbbell on the floor now, King was backing away from the mirror, his palms up in front of him. 'This is insane. I'm no thinking aboot this. I'm no even thinking aboot thinking aboot this. This is just . . . no!'

'Good for you,' said the mirror. 'I knew the decent streak was in ye. And look on the bright side . . . if ye learn to accept being the second-bonniest man in Glesga, folk might start praising ye for yer modesty.'

Percy Pig was blethering away on his mobile in the comfort of his straw house.

'Och, he just wants to show aff his fancy new brick hoose, like he's pure better than us or that! Still, it's been *days* since we had a party, so I'm going. How about you? . . . Haud on a second, somebody's at the door.'

The pig went to the door and called, 'Who is it?'

'Good evening, little pig,' said the voice on the other side of the door, in a velvety, upper-class English accent, which sang of a gentleness altogether missing from the bearer's nature. 'Might I trouble you to let me in?'

The pig, seeing through the peephole that the visitor was none other than the Big, Bad Wolf, replied, 'No, by the hair o' my chinny-chin-chin, by the way.'

The Wolf answered, 'I see. Then you leave me no option, I'm afraid, but to huff and puff and blow your house down.'

And he huffed. And he puffed. And he blew the house down!

Then he laughed to himself as the poor pig fled.

CHAPTER 2

'Can yous at least haud the stepladder?' pleaded Ella, scrubbing the ceiling furiously and becoming more and more worried about her balance.

Kara and Clara were waiting for their nails to dry and talking about boys.

'We're far too busy,' insisted Kara.

'And you're not scrubbing hard enough. Put some elbow grease into it!' added Clara.

'Stupid girl! Can't do anything by herself. Anyway . . . what were we talking about?'

'Harry Charmaine,' said Clara.

'Oh, yes,' said Kara. 'He is dreamy! He does have a rather . . . coarse turn of phrase – tends to revert to talking Scottish and that – but a good wife should be able to train that out of him!'

'He does have a rather . . . shapely bottom, doesn't he?'

'Oh, Clara, you are wicked!' cried Kara, giggling wildly. 'Still, one cannae help but notice these things.'

Ella dropped her scrubbing brush and climbed down the ladder to get to it.

'Klutz!' cried Kara.

'She can't do anything right,' sneered Clara.

'Normal people don't scrub ceilings!' insisted Ella, furiously.

'Neither do we!' said Kara, and both ugly sisters chuckled.

'I'm going now,' said Ella, more boldly than she usually dared. 'I'm already late for school.'

'You will come straight home?' said Kara. 'We need you to finish that ceiling tonight, because you need to bath the dogs tomorrow.'

'I've got work experience.'

'Very well,' said Kara. 'As long as you make sure the ceiling sparkles tonight. And we'll be sure to lock your mattress in the basement, in case you're tempted to go to bed before it's done!'

Ella left, without a word.

'Good afternoon, and welcome to *The Reggie King Show*,' said King, giving his best smile to the camera. 'Today we're going to be looking at the real-life Hogwarts; how one school in Glasgow is teaching magic to its pupils. Church leaders say it's a step too far.

'But first . . . we've all heard of the adventures of Scottish pirate Robert MacGuffin. But how much of them are true and how much is myth? I'm joined by Colin McGarth, expert in piratology, who claims that MacGuffin's treasure may be buried somewhere in Glasgow.

'Now, Colin . . . buried treasure, in Glasgow? It's the stuff of boys' adventure tales, surely?'

'Well,' said McGarth, straightening his tie and clearing his throat, trying his best to look serious through his thick, black spectacles. 'We know that there was a successful pirate called Robert MacGuffin, and that he did steal a lot more treasure than has been accounted for. We also know that he did bury his treasure at various ports around the world, and that Glasgow was one of his last ports of call before he was captured and hanged in Edinburgh.

'We've recently uncovered his diary, which is a most remarkable find, and has been verified by experts, which suggests that he had, in fact, planned to retire from piracy and settle in Glasgow with his fiancée. So I think it's very likely that there may be treasure here.'

'I don't suppose you have any idea of its precise location? I mean, if you did, you surely wouldn't be sat here talking to me!'

McGarth laughed nervously. 'Yes, that's true. We don't know exactly where the treasure is, but we're uncovering new clues all the time, and I believe there will be a big find in the next few years, and I'm confident it will be right here in Glasgow.'

King laughed and addressed the camera. 'Well, get out your spades, folks, because you could have pirate treasure buried in your garden! And remember when you find it, you heard about it first on the Reggie King show!'

Ella was busy taking coffee orders from the people in the office.

'I'll get that,' came a kind voice from behind her.

She turned to find herself looking into the gorgeous smile of Reggie King himself.

'About time I did some actual work in here,' the TV star chuckled. 'You go sit in my office. There's a couple of things I'd like to talk to you about.'

So Ella sat in King's private office, looking nervously around her: at the awards in the cabinet; at the neatly piled papers on the desk; at the comfy-looking leather swivel chair.

Here she was, about to speak to one of Scotland's top celebrities, who wanted to see her – wee Ella McCinder – for some reason. Of course, she'd rather be waiting to speak to Harry Charmaine, but maybe King could arrange that.

But what if she'd done something wrong? What if he was going to tell her to get out and never come back? Then she'd never get to meet Harry. Worse still, she'd have no excuse to avoid her foster family after school.

Excitement and dread filled her belly. For want of anything better to do with so much adrenaline, she began spinning in the chair.

'Having fun?' came a voice from the door.

Ella stopped dead to find herself face-to-face with Reggie King. She went bright red.

King laughed. 'Don't worry about it. That's what burly-chairs are for. Just between us, I cannae resist the occasional burl myself!'

Ella giggled as King sat on the desk.

'How are you, Ella?' asked King.

'Fine, thank you, Mr King.'

'Call me Reggie. I don't want you treating me like I'm a celebrity, or I'm yer boss. I'm a mate, that's all. Okay?'

Ella nodded, relaxing a little, though she was still chewing her hair nervously.

'Good,' said King with his kindest smile. 'Now tell me the truth. How are you, really? And don't say "fine", because you're not fine.'

Ella shrugged.

'Ella,' said King, 'I believe in looking after my staff. I don't care if you're just on work experience, I want to treat you like I would treat anyone else who works here. And if somebody here is maybe going through a rough time, or is upset about something, I want to know about it. I want to help.'

Ella nibbled her knuckles. 'It's nothing I can't handle.'

'I know, I know,' said King. 'It's family business. You're embarrassed about it. You don't want anybody to know. I was the same when I was in care.'

Ella's eyes went wide. 'How . . . ?'

King laughed. 'Don't look so shocked. I'm a journalist. I can find out stuff. I know you've been taken into care. I know your mum's in jail, and I know the family you're staying with is treating you like dirt.'

Ella seemed stunned, then thoughtful. Tears leaked from her eyes.

'Oh, there, there,' said King. 'You cry as much as you need to.'

Ella sniffed, 'Thank you. I never thought I'd find anyone I could talk to about this.'

'Och, don't mention it, I'm here to help,' insisted King. 'You do believe me, don't you?' he said, holding her face in his hands. 'That I only want to help you?'

'Aye,' said Ella.

'Do you trust me, Ella?'

'Aye,' said Ella.

'Good,' said King. 'You see, some of my friends are social workers and

[15]

it's entirely possible I could manage to get you shifted to a family I know personally, who would be kind to you. I also have friends who are judges, lawyers . . . I'm a very powerful and influential man. I bet you thought I was just a pretty face! There's an outside chance I could even help get your mother out early. How does that grab ye?'

Ella gasped. 'That would be wonderful!'

'Easy, now,' he said. 'Now don't get yer hopes up, I'm no promising anything. Now . . . what were you hoping to get out of doing work experience here, hmm? What made you choose the Reggie King show?'

'Um . . . because I'm such a big fan of yours.'

King laughed and clapped her on the shoulder. 'Now, don't you lie to me, Ella. I can always tell. You don't need to flatter me. Now, come on . . . what are you really after, here?'

'Well . . .' Ella squirmed and wriggled in her seat. 'I . . . to be honest I was sort of hoping to meet Harry Charmaine . . .'

'Oh, aye,' beamed King. 'Good old Harry Charming. He's an awfae decent lad, even if he does play for Celtic, and no much older than you. Actually, it's funny you should mention him . . . he was in the office earlier going over some notes for the interview next week – you wouldnae have seen him – but he says to me, "Reggie, who's that beautiful young lady going aboot there?" I think he was talking about you!'

Ella grabbed her now-red face in both her hands. 'You're kidding me on!'

'No, I swear! I wouldnae joke aboot something like this. He's a wee bit shy, so he asked me if I could maybe introduce you. How would you feel about maybe having dinner with him sometime next week?'

Ella was breathing hard, speechless. 'That would be . . .' she managed when she finally got her breath back, 'that would be, like . . . wow!'

'Aye, I'll manage that. So, ye feeling a wee bit better?'

'Aye,' said Ella. 'Thank you so much.'

'Don't mention it. See, between you and me, I think you're someone really, really special. Someone I can really rely on, you know? I need people like that working for me.'

[16]

'Thank you.'

'Do you trust me, Ella? I'm being deadly serious now. Do you trust me?'

She met his cold, hard stare, and for the first time since he had started putting her at her ease, she felt afraid. Still she answered, 'Aye.'

'Would you do anything for me? Absolutely anything?'

'Aye,' she replied.

'Now don't you answer a question like that lightly,' said King. 'Would you do absolutely anything for me? I need you to be absolutely sincere.'

'Aye,' said Ella. 'Aye, I would.'

'What I ask will no be easy,' said King.

'What is it you want me to do?' Ella replied.

King handed her a photograph of a beautiful man with white hair, soft skin and a near-perfect smile.

'Take a good look at that picture, Ella. What do you make of it?'

'He's gorgeous,' said Ella, without the slightest hesitation.

'Yes,' King echoed darkly, 'he is, isn't he? But don't let that fool you! This man is the heart of darkness in Glasgow. He is pure evil.'

'You're joking, right?'

'I wish I were! His name is Karl White, known as "Snowy". He must be destroyed.'

Ella laughed. It was so ridiculous! It had to be a joke. It had to be one of those hidden camera shows. 'You cannae be serious.'

He grabbed her roughly by the shoulders, shook her and roared: 'I'VE NEVER BEEN SO SERIOUS ABOUT ANYTHING IN MY LIFE!' He calmed down abruptly. 'I'm sorry. I didnae mean to frighten you, but you absolutely must take this seriously.' He pressed a knife into her hand. 'On the back of the photo is the address of a flat in Partick, where he lives. The Number 62 bus stops right outside. There's nae secure entry system or anything. Just walk up and knock the door. When he answers . . . don't even look up, or your courage will be gone. Just plunge the knife straight into him, and cut out his heart and bring it to me.'

Ella's head was spinning. She couldn't make any sense of any of this. She whispered, 'What if I refuse?'

'If you refuse you will have broken your promise. You'll have let me down, you'll have let yourself down, and you will have let all of Glasgow down.

'Moreover, if you refuse I will be disappointed and that means I will make your life a living hell. Not all young people in care get put with families. Some get put in secure units where you'll be the only one there who's no a hardened criminal; where they don't bother flushing the plug before they stuff yer heid doon the lavvy! And that's just the staff! They'd make your ugly foster sisters look like the Care Bears!

'And as for yer maw . . . well, I can pull strings to help her get early release . . . or I can pull strings to make sure she suffers inside! And I mean *suffers*.

'I'm a very powerful man. I am Reginald King, and Reginald King always gets what he wants.'

He cupped her face in his hands. 'I don't want to sound harsh. But I need to impress upon you how serious this is. There's no one else I can turn to, Ella. No one else I can trust. I promise you I can get you together with Harry Charming. I promise you I can make your life better, but you have to trust me and you have to do what I ask. Will you?'

She felt sick. She felt humiliated. She felt hatred and love towards King all at once. And through it all, she felt herself nodding. 'Yes. Yes I will.'

'Good girl. Now don't stop and think about it or your courage will be gone. Go now!'

Nodding frantically and tucking the knife under her armpit, Ella left the building.

The soft-faced, white-haired, sparkly-eyed Karl 'Snowy' White sat alone in his flat, drinking tea and reading his comic books. There was a knock at the door.

He carefully bookmarked his comic with a sweetie wrapper from the floor, hoisted himself up and made his way to the front door.

[18]

But when he opened it, he heard footsteps running away, and a sound echoing through the close that he took for giggling, but could have been sobbing.

'Welcome to Glasgow,' he mused, then closed the door and went back to his comic.

CHAPTER 3

'Haw, mirror,' said King, thoughtfully. 'I don't suppose there's any chance the treasure of MacGuffin actually is in Glasgow?'

'Not a chance, Mr King, but a certainty.'

'Now that is interesting,' replied King. 'And would you happen to know its exact location?'

'Aye,' said the mirror, sounding slightly hurt to be doubted. 'It's in Easterhoose.'

King punched the air. 'Ya dancer! And I, Reggie King, King of Scotland, shall dig it up *live* on the Reggie King show, and my beautiful face will be on the front pages of newspapers across the globe!'

'That would be a fine achievement,' said the mirror. 'Too bad it's no gonnae happen.'

'What?' growled the TV star.

'There is an obstacle in your way,' the mirror informed him coolly.

'What kind of obstacle?'

'I'm afraid the treasure of MacGuffin lies directly under a stick house, where two little pigs dwell, and they can't be shifted for any money.'

'Couldn't we dig down near the treasure, then burrow along horizontally?'

'Not without doing major structural damage to surrounding buildings,' said the mirror. 'It is in the middle of a housing scheme.'

'Well,' said King, 'I'll give any price they ask for their wee stick hoose, then knock it doon, and dig. Simple.'

'I told you,' the mirror explained patiently, 'Money willnae dae it. Pigs are notorious for being stubborn, and they'll no be shifted except by force.'

King's features darkened. 'Then by God, I'll shift them by force!'

'Excellent choice, Mr King,' said the mirror. 'I'm happy to recommend the services of a young entrepreneur known locally as the Big, Bad Wolf.'

Jack had been spending a lot of time at Jill's flat since her break-up with King. He felt he should cheer her up with pizza and Scrabble, and make sure she was alright. That's what brothers were for, after all.

One fateful Scrabble-and-pizza night was interrupted by a knock at the door.

'I'll get it,' said Jill, and found herself face-to-face with a frantic Ella.

'H-hi, I'm, I'm really sorry to . . . you probably don't even know . . . I only met ye the once, but ye seemed so, like . . . approachable, and I don't know who else to turn to, and I figured you'd maybe know him. He wanted me to kill this guy! I . . . my maw . . . he . . . promised me Harry and . . . I had a knife and . . .' she broke down.

'Come on in,' said Jill, wrapping a comforting arm around her. She didn't understand much of what the girl had said, but she clearly needed help. 'This is my brother, Jack.'

'Hi,' said Jack.

'I feel so embarrassed coming here,' said Ella, 'and I know ye're gonnae think I'm a pure psycho or that, but I just didnae know anywhere else I could turn.' She laughed. 'You probably don't even know who I am, do you?'

'Of course I do!' Jill told her kindly. 'You're the work experience lass who found my Partick Thistle mug when I lost it in Reggie's office and brought it back to me. That mug means a lot to me, so I'd never forget you!'

'Aye, I remember that,' said Ella. 'You were so nice to me.'

'She's nice to everyone,' said Jack. 'Just a great big ball of nice.'

'So, you're a Thistle fan, then?' asked Ella, glad of a change of subject.

'Aye, she is, but I try and treat her like she was normal,' said Jack.

Jill chuckled. 'This yin and Maw are Rangers daft, but I cannae be doing wi' all the sectarian rubbish that goes wi' Celtic and Rangers, so I switched to Partick when I was about fifteen.'

The three of them talked about football for a while, as Ella became gradually calmer.

'You didnae come here to talk football, though, did you?' said Jill.

Ella swallowed hard. 'Could we . . . talk privately?'

'Aye. Come on oot to the balcony.'

They were twenty floors up, and the view Jill's modest balcony presented of the city was quite magnificent. Surrounded on all sides by majestic hills, Glasgow's gargantuan bodyguards, the city spread out before them was arranged in curves, never a straight line. Where the amber sunlight hit the mists rising off the River Clyde, a watercolour collage was created that one never finds anywhere else: the colour of Glasgow.

Ella told Jill about her foster family. 'That's why when Mr King told me he was in care, I felt . . . I dunno . . . kinda connected or that.'

Jill chuckled. 'He tellt you he was in care?'

'Wasn't he?'

Jill shook her head. 'By his standards, he had a perfect upbringing: raised in the palm of his middle-class parents' hands, wanting for nothing. Part of his problem is he's never learned to deal wi' no getting what he wants.'

'It's hard for me to tell you all of this, because you're his ex-girlfriend *and* you'll never believe me. You'll think I'm a pure nutter or that.'

Jill squeezed her shoulder. 'You'd be surprised what I'll believe,' then she listened intently while Ella told the story.

'He seemed so nice,' whispered Ella, finally.

'People who want to hurt you often do.'

'I was gonnae dae it! It sounds mad, but I was actually gonnae dae like he said!'

'Och, don't you dwell on that,' said Jill. 'You're a good person, and you've done nothing wrang. You didnae hurt anyone. You came to me instead, and that was the right thing to dae. We don't get judged for what we were gonnae dae, you know.'

Ella nodded. 'Thanks. Another thing . . . he said Snowy is evil or something . . . what's that all aboot?'

Jill shook her head. 'That's not it. By all accounts, Reggie doesnae have a lot against evil. Tell me, you saw a photie o' Snowy . . . would you say he's attractive?'

'Oh, yes!'

'More attractive than Reggie?'

Ella bounced her head from side to side, mentally comparing the two faces. 'Aye. Aye, it's a close thing, but . . . aye, Snowy's better looking.'

'That'll be it, then.'

'What? He wants to kill Snowy for being better looking? That's like the stupidest motive ever!'

'To you and me, aye, but to somebody like Reg, who's always had everything his ain way, and who can't bear the thought of no being the bonniest man in Glesga . . .'

They stood in silence for a while. Jill leaned over the railing and stretched her hand over in front of her, as though she could grab the whole city in one hand.

'There's a lot more going on here than you realise, Ella. You've tellt me your secrets, so I'll tell you mine.'

There was a long pause. 'I'm listening,' said Ella, gently.

'It's a hard thing to say out loud . . .' She spun to look Ella in the eye. 'I'm a witch.'

Ella didn't flinch. 'Ye mean, like, ye believe in magic and that?'

'I don't just believe in it. I see it. I feel it. I use it. And this city is full of it.

'There's two Glasgows, Ella. There's the wan ye walk through every day and never really think aboot; where ye live, work, go clubbing, take abuse fae bus drivers and laugh at drunk people.

'Then there's the other Glasgow, which lives in a' the wee alleyways that don't seem to go anywhere; a' the amazing architecture folk never see because they'll no look up; a' the treasures this city likes to hide in plain sight, like Otago Lane, or the market off Byres Road, or Crookston Castle. Most folk will only ever see the Magical Glasgow oot the corner of their eye, and forget aboot it right away.

'Me, I live in that other Glasgow, where anything's possible. Look!' she threw her arms wide, taking in the whole glory of the city.'How can anyone look at that and no see magic?'

'Aye,' said Ella, smiling softly.

'When you can see the magic in this city, nothing is as simple as it appears,' Jill explained.'Reggie possesses a mirror; a magical mirror, which talks to him.'

'I believe you,' said Ella.

Jill smiled.'Aye. That's the advantage of meeting other folk who know that extraordinary things happen in the ordinary world!'

'This mirror . . . it, or the demon inside it, or whatever is at work here . . . it's got some very powerful dark magic inside it. And whatever it's been saying to Reggie seems to be having an effect.'

'So it's no really his fault?'

'Oh, he's responsible as much as the mirror is. He still has free will, and he still knows right fae wrang. You've got to be running pretty low on morals afore you'll let a mirror talk you into murder. But it . . . has influence.'

They stared out at the now sunset-silhouetted city. It was getting late, and there was a bit of a chill in the breeze.

'This is all my fault,' whispered Jill, leaning over the balcony and spilling tears all the way down to the street below.

'How can it be your fault?' said Ella.

'Because I gave it to him.'

Ella hadn't expected to be the one comforting Jill and didn't really know what to say. 'You werenae to know,' Ella said.

'Oh, but I should have! You can't put dark magic that powerful into the hands of someone like him. But . . . well, it wasnae a gift given out of kind-ness . . .'

'How'd you mean?'

Jill drew a deep breath and crossed her arms: this was clearly not a subject she was eager to discuss. 'The mirror said things . . . horrible things. How I was fat and ugly and no one would want me. How Reggie only went out with me because he felt sorry for me. How I was worthless and I'd be better off dead. The mirror . . . it has some kind of magic that can get right inside your head. I . . . ended up trying to kill myself.

'Once I'd recovered, I kept away from the mirror for a while. I was starting to calm doon and see sense a bit . . . I realised what it was doing to me. Now, I've never thought much of the way I look, which I thought was why the mirror was so dangerous for me. I figured for someone like King, who pure fancied himself, it might just teach him some humility. So I gave it to him.'

'But it didnae work . . .'

Jill shook her head. 'I was naive and had nae clue how dark magic really works. How I think it works is . . . I think whatever your biggest failing is, your biggest flaw, it'll exaggerate it a hundred times, and start finding ways to use it against you.'

'So wi' you it was, like, your low self-image and that. Wi' Mr King, it's his vanity.'

'Aye. Something like that. So you see that it's really quite important to me that nae harm comes to anyone on account of that mirror.'

'Aye,' said Ella, softly.

'Listen, I'll keep this between us if that's what ye want . . . but I'd like to talk it over wi' my brother Jack. He's aye there for me, whatever I'm going through, and if ye trust me ye can trust him.'

'Aye, okay,' said Ella.

'Then let's take this conversation into the living room. It's freezing oot here!'

*　　*　　*

'I'm gonnae go roond to his bit right now to put his heid in for him!' Jack exclaimed, on learning of King's villainy.

'Glad I didnae gie the mirror to you,' Jill muttered under her breath. 'Look,' she said aloud, 'let's just stop and think aboot this, eh?'

'There's a time for stopping and thinking,' insisted Jack, 'and there's a time for dishing oot severe doings!'

'Right,' Jill sighed. 'We'll have nae mair "severe doings" talk, okay? 'Cause it'll no dae anyone any good. Now, I've got an idea how to handle this, but it'll no be easy.'

Jack and Ella leaned in closer, listening intently.

'I know a place we can send Snowy where he'll be safe. We just need to stall Reggie long enough to get him there.'

'How?' said Ella.

'I need you to be really brave, here. I have a friend, works as a stock assistant at a butcher; always winding me up aboot being vegetarian. He works night shift, we should be able to catch him fairly soon. We'll ask him for the heart of a cow.'

Ella went pale. 'I'm gonnae be sick.'

Jill sat next to her and rubbed her back. 'I know it's really horrid to think about.'

Jack brought a bucket, but Ella didn't need it.

'After you've done that, I'm guessing Reggie's no gonnae be pleased when he finds oot, so you need to stay safe just in case. Get a taxi to and from school. Don't worry, I'll pay for it. Don't go anywhere except school unless it's here, or I know exactly where you are. Don't leave school grounds – school dinners for you, I'm afraid. Make sure yer mobile's charged at all times, so's ye can phone me if there's any trouble.'

Ella nodded slowly, shaking all over.

'That's a lot to ask of a sixteen-year-old,' Jack piped in. 'Giving up her social life, eating school dinners, living in fear. Why don't I just nip roond to King's bit with a baseball bat and ask him to desist?'

Jill sighed loudly and massaged her temples. 'Jack, I'm gonnae say something you'll hate me for saying, and I've been trying no to say it, but you're determined to make me say it . . .'

'What's that then?'

'Reggie can take you.'

Jack snorted. 'That big Jessie?'

'That "Big Jessie,"' said Jill, 'works out more than you fart. You go after him with a baseball bat, he will put you in hospital, and the papers will be full of "HAVE-A-GO HERO KING TACKLES PSYCHO INTRUDER." Then he will put you in jail, and the papers will be full of how yer sentence isnae long enough. And because I'm your sister and his ex, they'll be forever hounding me, and I can dae withoot that. So gie it a rest wi' this baseball bat rubbish, okay?'

Jack folded his arms and said nothing.

Jill squeezed Ella's shoulder. 'I wish there was a better way of doing this. And if you walk away, you'll probably stay oot o' harm's way, but it's touch-and-go whether I can save Snowy.' She looked deep into Ella's eyes. 'Look, it's no fair me asking you to do this. You didnae ask to get involved in any o' this. So if you want to go hame and forget it, I don't blame you.'

Ella smiled and shrugged. 'It's no every day ye get the chance to be a hero, is it?'

A knock at the door of King's luxury West End apartment interrupted his press-ups.

He opened it to the trembling form of Ella. Her face was pale and her eyes were red.

'Ella, my dear,' said King, smiling pleasantly. 'Please come in.'

'I-I cannae stay long,' whispered Ella. She was shaking violently. 'I did what ye asked.' She handed him a tin box.

King opened it and closed it almost at once, trying not to let Ella see that his stomach was turned by what he saw.

'Your courage is extraordinary.' He hugged her tightly, whilst trying not to let her bloodstained hands touch him. 'Can I give ye a lift anywhere?'

'No, I'll make my own way thanks,' said Ella.

'Ye sure?'

'Aye.'

'Can I no get ye a drink or anything?'

'No, I need to go,' said Ella. 'But . . . all that stuff ye promised . . .'

'Good as done, darling. Good as done!'

Ella gave a tiny smile, then turned away and left.

King closed the door after her, saying, 'The cold-blooded little witch actually did it. I like her.' He addressed the tin. 'Alas, poor Snowy. I am sorry it had to be this way, but there can only be wan bonniest man in Glesga, and it's no gonnae be some jumped-up, white-haired teuchter.'

He stuck the tin in the fridge and went back to his push-ups.

A knock at the door of Snowy's poky wee flat in Partick interrupted his comic book-reading.

He opened it to be confronted by a vision of loveliness unlike anything he had ever seen before; a full-bodied woman with hair so soft a man could never get tired stroking it, chocolate-coloured eyes that spoke of intelligence and genuine, limitless warmth, and a smooth-skinned, chubby face, full of the sort of lines you only get from smiling.

There was no smile on that beautiful face now, though. Only worry.

'Snowy White?' said Jill.

'Yes,' said Snowy. 'How did you . . . ?'

'You're in very grave danger. You know Reggie King, from the telly?'

'Aye, whatever you might have heard, we do have tellies in the Highlands.'

'He wants to kill you.'

'What?'

Jill explained the situation as briefly as she could and ushered him into a taxi.

He wanted to complain. He wanted to resist. But how could he argue with so lovely a lassie?

Besides, his gut was telling him that her words were true, and Snowy White trusted his gut implicitly.

So in the space of a few crazy minutes, his life was changed forever.

Later that evening, a second knock at King's door interrupted his exercises.

'What now?' he grumbled and answered the door. 'Jill. What a lovely surprise.'

'I want my mirror back,' said Jill.

'Mirror? What mirr – oh, *that* mirror. Jill, I don't want to get into a fight wi' ye, but I really do think ye've got a bit of a cheek, after you destroyed so much of my property; stuff that was actually mine. You're lucky I didnae phone the polis on ye.'

Jill swallowed hard. 'I'm sorry aboot that. I was angry. I'll pay ye back for any damages.'

'Jill, the only reason you can afford to pay me back is because ye flogged all the shiny beads I ever gave ye. Which would've come to a fair wee dollop o' cash, by the way: I was good to you. Secondly, dae I look like I'm short of a bob or two? But ye cannae have the mirror back. It's irreplaceable.'

'Reggie, please,' pleaded Jill. 'Can you no see what that thing's turning you into?'

'I'll tell you what I see, my dear Jillipoos,' said King, trying to cup her face in his hands. She backed off. 'I see a silly lassie whose boyfriend broke up wi' her, and who cannae cope wi' the fact that it's over.'

'Don't call me that stupid pet name!' she hissed. 'I've always hated that! And just to remind you . . . I broke up wi' you.'

'Read the newspapers,' said King, 'if ye cannae mind who dumped who.'

'Who dumped *whom*,' she corrected him viciously. 'I don't need the papers to tell me. I was there!'

'Aye, but you're no thinking straight. Seriously, Jill . . . look at you. And look at me. Then ask yersel' who lost mair when it ended.'

Jill delivered him a hefty boot between the legs, causing him to collapse in a heap. 'I'll get that mirror off you, wan way or another.'

[29]

'I'm warning you, Jill!' King growled from the floor. 'If I have to get a restraining order oot against you, every journalist on my mobile gets to know aboot it! Your life willnae be worth living! Don't you mess wi' the King!'

'I tellt ye!' insisted Peter Pig. 'Did I no tell ye? It's a stick hoose ye want to build for comfort and security. But no . . . you said straw would dae ye just fine.'

'Aye, alright, Peter,' said Percy. 'You don't have to keep going on aboot it.'

'I know I don't have to,' said Peter. 'I just like it. You're a pure dafty, by the way.'

Their argument was interrupted by a knock at the door.

Peter could see by looking through the peephole that it was none other than the Big, Bad Wolf.

'It's the Wolf!' hissed Peter. 'But don't worry. He'll no get in.'

'Good afternoon, little pigs,' called the Wolf, whose big ears gave him no trouble in hearing their conversation. 'Do, please, let me in.'

'No by the hair on oor chinny-chin-chins, by the way!' the pigs replied.

'I see,' said the Wolf. 'Then you have none but yourselves to blame when I huff, and I puff, and I blow your house down!'

And he huffed! And he puffed! And he blew the house down!

Two little pigs emerged from the wreckage.

'What was that you were saying aboot stick hooses?' asked Percy.

When Ella came 'home', she was exhausted, and scrubbing the ceiling was the last thing on her mind.

Reaching her bedroom, she found her mattress and bedclothes were gone, just as Kara had threatened.

Lying down on the metal springs of her bed, she cried herself to sleep.

CHAPTER 4

The taxi let Snowy off several hundred yards from where he was going. Jill had been adamant that no one else should see where he went.

'But how should I know where to go?' said Snowy.

'Just go where your feet take you,' said Jill. 'Trust me, anyone who needs to find this place will.'

Snowy felt so stupid. He felt tricked. He felt alone. More than that, he felt afraid, because he may have been simply led to a secluded spot to be murdered.

With that chilling thought, he picked up a large stick . . .

How would he find his way in the dark? He was reasonably certain he was somewhere in Calderglen Country Park. Could he just follow the road back the way the taxi had come? It could be miles. Would that take him to the road where he could get the Number 20 bus back to Glasgow?

His gut feeling that Jill had been telling the truth was still with him . . . but had he simply been blinded by her beauty?

Suddenly, the dark colours of the night seemed to warp around him in a way he could not quite explain; as though he had stepped into a bubble and out of reality as he knew it.

An old granite house stood in front of him where none had been before.

'This must be the place,' he said to himself, knocking tentatively at the door.

The gnarled, hunch-backed hag who opened the creaking door had greenish-grey, flaking, leathery skin, one giant red eye the size of a cricket ball, and one tiny black one the size of a raisin. An unfashionable bonnet partially concealed hair that looked like copper wire, and her clothes were beige and torn.

'What dae ye want?' she snarled.

'I, um . . .' Snowy hardly knew how to respond. He decided to stick rigidly to the script. 'Jill sent me.'

'Oh,' said the creature. 'Suppose ye best come in.'

She led him to a damp, dark living area with rubbish, clothes and dirty dishes strewn over the floor.

Four further creatures crowded round him.

'These are my family,' said the one who had answered the door. 'This is Glaikit.'

Glaikit was a big, hairy man, with close-set eyes, seeming in his posture more ape than man. He had a bulbous, green nose and pointy teeth.

'This is Dagger.'

Dagger seemed like a normal – if oddly dressed and slightly pale – human being . . . until he took his hands out from behind his back, to reveal that they were not hands at all but sharp knives.

Dagger approached Snowy, sniffed him, and with a horrid, disdainful grimace, declared, 'Human!'

Snowy flinched.

'Forgive Dagger,' said the strangest of them all, a green-skinned creature who might have been a reptile but for walking upright. He had yellow eyes and two great nostrils where one would expect to see a nose. 'Years of isolation from what you would call *normal* people has had a right queer effect on us a'. In his case, it's eroded his manners! I am known as Dragonman, which I find delightfully quaint!'

Dragonman extended a scaly hand, which Snowy shook tentatively.

'This is Nono,' said the hag.

Nono was a short creature with no discernable facial features other than his huge, oval eyes. His head spun round and round independently of his body and he cried, 'Nononononononononononononononononononononono!'

'He does that when he gets excited. Ye get used to it. And me . . . I'm Crabbit. We don't mind being called the Freaks, the Mutants, the Mutant Freaks, the Five Freaks, the Five Mutants or the Five Mutant Freaks.'

'It's a pleasure,' said Snowy, swallowing hard. 'I'm Snowy, by the way.'

'Whatever,' said Crabbit. 'See Jill? We owe her everything. Whatever, whoever is after ye, it won't find ye here, but keep this close to you, just in case.' She flung him a crystal ball. 'When that glows red-hot, it means that danger is near. Jill gied us that and it's never let us doon, probably because danger's never been near.'

She then kicked a time-battered two-seat sofa, causing dust to rise from it. 'You sleep here. Don't get up in the middle of the night, don't leave the lavvy seat up, and don't – whatever ye do, *don't* – tidy up!'

'Are you alright?' Jack asked his sister. 'You're looking a bit . . . glum.'

'Just thinking aboot Ella,' said Jill, sadly. 'She's having a really hard time of it. I just wish . . . I just wish there was something we could dae for her, you know? Make her life a wee bit easier. . .' Suddenly she grinned. 'Maybe there is!'

She flicked her mobile phone out and quickly poked in a number. 'Oh, hi, Aunt Heather, it's Jill here . . . Och, cannae complain. Listen, is my Fairy Godmaw aboot?'

'Good afternoon, and welcome to *The Reggie King Show*,' King said to the camera. He was wearing a hard hat and had to speak up over the roar of diggers and drills.

'We've got quite a special show for you today, as we can reveal exclusively that a team of scientists believes it has found the elusive treasure of the Scottish pirate, Robert MacGuffin, under an ordinary courtyard of Glasgow's Easterhouse estate.

'I'm joined now by pirate expert Colin McGarth. Colin, even I can feel the palpable excitement in the air at this time. I can only imagine what it must be doing to you.'

McGarth looked as if he didn't know whether to jump up and down or lie down. He made jerky hand-gestures as he spoke, and his eyes were bulging with excitement. 'Yes, Reggie, I . . . we've been searching for this treasure for many, many years, and most people have been highly sceptical about its existence . . . but, you just never know! Last week I was on your show saying "maybe someday", and today . . . well, someday is today. It's the most amazing feeling in the world, and it's just . . . it's just indescribable. That's the only word to describe it.'

With a click, King's face appeared on the old black and white TV in the Freaks' living room.

'And if you've just joined us,' King was saying, 'this is The Big Dig, live with The Reggie King Show, where we reckon there's a good chance we're actually going to find the MacGuffin pirate's treasure!'

'That's him,' said Snowy. 'That's the man who wants to kill me.'

'Really?' said Crabbit. 'Why?'

'And I think any minute now . . .' King was saying.

'He thinks I'm better looking than him, apparently.'

The crane on the screen was pulling up something large and heavy from a deep hole in the ground. 'Yes, we definitely have something,' said King.

Crabbit snorted. 'All normals look the same to me.'

'Well, this is an historic occasion,' said King.

'A historic occasion!' Crabbit growled at the screen. 'H is a consonant! I really hate that.'

'As you can see,' King went on, 'that's definitely a chest of some kind . . . Colin, what are your thoughts at this time?'

'I'm just . . . speechless,' said McGarth.

'Couldn't have put it better myself,' said King. 'You're watching The Big Dig live with The Reggie King Show, and we have unearthed something quite substantial . . .'

'Look at him with his hard hat,' remarked Snowy. 'He looks like Bob the Builder!'

Snowy could have never anticipated the Freaks' reaction to his off-the-cuff witticism; they howled and roared with laughter (all except Nono, who spun his head faster than ever, crying, 'Nonononononononononononono!' with the tone and rhythm of laughter).

Snowy wondered for a moment if they were being sarcastic, but they seemed genuine.

When the laughter had died down, Snowy said, 'It wasn't that funny . . .' which started the laughter off all over again.

'We haven't laughed like that since we moved in here!' cried Crabbit, slapping his shoulder. 'But this doesnae mean we like you.'

This is it, thought King. *This is the moment I was born for.*

'And now, this historic moment, the moment we've all been waiting for, is here. The chest, thought to contain the treasure of the pirate MacGuffin, has been exhumed, and we're about to open it and take a look inside. Colin, what are your thoughts at this time?'

Colin McGarth seemed to be having trouble breathing. 'Please,' he breathed. 'Just open it!'

King laughed. 'Well, Colin McGarth can't wait and I certainly can't blame him. I'm sure it's the same for you at home . . .'

The mahogany chest was as solid as the day it had been buried. It was the size of a baby's cot, decorated with elegant carvings of ships and weapons, and held shut by a rusty lock.

King carelessly inserted a wrench and tore open the box which had been shut for 260 years.

What did he see?

It took his mind a moment to catch up with his vision.

His eyes were almost burned by sun's reflection on the contents of the chest.

There was gold.

There was silver.

There were precious jewels sparkling loudly in every imaginable colour.

'Well,' said King, 'There you have it. The lost treasure of Robert MacGuffin, unearthed live on *The Reggie King Show*. Never, in my wildest imagination, could I have envisioned a sight like this. Colin, what are your thoughts at this time?'

Colin McGarth was speechless.

'Well,' said King, trying to keep it going. 'I think the next step is to . . . get an inventory together and try and get some idea the value of this treasure. I imagine it will be quite a lot.'

'Priceless,' whispered McGarth.

'So, Colin,' said King, 'what are your thoughts at this historic moment?'

'We found it!' McGarth roared, punching the air.

'Yes,' said King. 'We have, indeed, found it. You're watching *The Big Dig* live with *The Reggie King Show*, and if you've just joined us, you're watching history in the making, because we have just unearthed the pirate's treasure, right here in Easterhouse. Isn't that magnificent?'

He moved forward, as though to touch the treasure . . . but before he got the chance, a great, booming voice came from within the shaft that had been dug.

'WHO IS IT THAT WAD DAUR LAY THEIR HAUNDS ON MY TREASURE?'

King unplugged his microphone and hissed to his assistant, 'Whoever's messing aboot, get them to knock it off. This is live on air!' He plugged in his microphone and turned to camera. 'Ah . . . we seem to be experiencing technical difficulties, I apologise for any reduction of your viewing pleasure . . .'

'I'M NAE TECHNICAL DIFFICULTY,' boomed the voice. 'I'M THE GHAIST O' RAB MACGUFFIN . . . AND YOU, REGINALD KING, WHO SET THE BIG BAD WOLF ON TWA INNOCENT PIGS TO LAY YER GREEDY WEE FINGERS ON MY TREASURE . . . I KEN WEEL WHO YOU ARE!'

A queer, purplish mist rose from the great big hole in the ground. When it cleared, there stood – all seven feet of him – a see-through spectre of

Robert MacGuffin. His black, greasy hair stuck out in all directions; half his face was missing from the wounds of battle; when he spoke, his beard parted to reveal blood-stained teeth, for he was well known for rending his victims' flesh from bone with no other weapon. He wore the ragged clothes of a prisoner and there was a noose around his neck.

'YOU, KING, ARE A WORSE SCOUNDREL THAN ONY I SAILED THE SEAS WI'! AND I'VE SAILED WI' SOME UNCO WICKED MEN, I TELL YE! YOU, REGINALD KING, ARE A WORM! AND YE'LL NAE BE TACKING MY TREASURE FOR YER AIN PATHETIC NOTION O' GLORY! YOU THAT'S NEVER KNOWN THE BURN O' A CUTLASS OR MUSKET BALL UNDER YER SKIN, THAT WOULDNAE HAE A CLUE WHAT GLORY IS REALLY ABOOT!'

His roar conjured a vicious wind and a cutlass appeared in his ghostly hand, whose blade he thrust into King's body. Like the ghost, it was insubstantial and caused Reggie no injury, but the shiver it sent through him, as if his insides were suddenly made of snow, reduced King to a quivering wreck on the ground.

The spectre turned to the glistening treasure. 'AYE,' he said with a ghostly sigh. 'WAD THAT NO JUST GAR YER WEE HEART BURST WI' THE BEAUTY O' IT? NAE WONDER YE'D GANG TO SIC LENGTHS. BUT I FOUCHT, AYE, AND EVEN DIED FOR THAT, AND NAE LIVING HAUND SHALL TOUCH IT WHEN I'M DEID!'

With that, he brought his sword down upon the treasure chest. There was a flash of light, a rush of wind, then ghost and treasure were gone.

'Well, er . . .' King dragged himself to his feet and shook himself off, trying not to show what misery and terror had just overcome him. 'We don't know quite what just happened here on *The Big Dig* live, and of course we will keep you informed as soon as we know anything. Here's Caroline with the weather.'

In a dingy, poorly lit pub, beyond the reach of the smoking ban, the Big, Bad Wolf was meeting with his latest client.

'It's a dynamic and innovative scheme, which would be worth a lot to the local economy, and . . .'

'You're boring me,' the Wolf sharply interrupted the human. 'If you would be so kind . . . just tell me my part. It's all I need to know.'

'There's a house – home to three little pigs – right where we want to put our supermarket. Our ideal solution would be for the pigs to move out and us to knock the house down. We've offered them a very generous cash settlement, but they don't seem at all interested in money. I can't understand it!'

'Well, pigs are well-known for being pig-headed,' said the Wolf. 'Am I to understand that you are soliciting me to . . . use my powers of persuasion to change the pigs' minds about moving?'

'We would be most appreciative if you could achieve this, yes.'

The Wolf grinned hungrily. 'I, as you may have noticed, am not a pig. I'm very interested in money. You're aware of my rates?'

'Yes.'

'I won't be talked down in price.'

'I wouldn't dream of trying.'

'Then we have an accord?'

'Yes, we do.'

The Wolf chuckled to himself.

'What's so funny?' asked the businessman.

'Oh, nothing much. It's just that I've been dealing rather a lot with pigs of late. It's an extraordinary coincidence.'

'KING IN GHOST HOAX CONFUSION.' King read the headline and threw the newspaper angrily at the mirror. 'ITC TO PROBE KING SHOW SPOOK HOAX.' He threw another paper. 'WHO YA GONNA CALL? NOT REGGIE!'

'Actually, that last one is rather amusing,' said the mirror.

'You didnae tell me I was liable to be attacked by the actual ghost of Robert MacGuffin!'

'You didnae ask.' Even with its lack of shoulders, the twisted face in the mirror managed to shrug.

[38]

'Not funny,' growled King. 'I'm not in a good mood. I'm still deeply shaken. That ghostly sword passing through me . . .' He shuddered, almost as though it were happening again.

'Poor baby,' said the mirror.

'I need cheering up,' insisted King, 'and I know just what will do the trick! So tell me . . . who's the bonniest man in Glesga?'

The mirror hesitated. 'Er . . . technically, you.'

'What do you mean, *technically*?' King exploded.

'Well, the young Snowy White, who is bonnier than you, is now living with some genetic misfits in Calderglen Country Park, East Kilbride. So you see, you are the bonniest man in Glasgow . . . but not the Greater Glasgow area.'

'I meant the bonniest *living* man,' sighed King. 'White is dead. His heart is in my fridge!'

'That's a coo's heart, ya mong!' spat the mirror. 'You've been duped.'

A silence as cold as death descended.

'White lives?'

'White lives.'

'No!' screamed the TV star. 'No! It cannae be!' He pointed an accusing finger. 'You assured me that McCinder would deliver!'

'Hey, I can see everything, but I cannae foresee everything,' said the mirror. 'Based on what we knew at the time, manipulating the McCinder wimp was your best chance.'

'I'm gonnae go to Calderglen right now and rip his pretty wee heart oot mysel'!'

'An excellent plan, Mr King . . . with just one tiny drawback.'

'Drawback? Don't you talk to me aboot drawbacks! I don't want to hear aboot drawbacks!'

'No one does, Mr King,' said the mirror, with infuriating calm. 'But where drawbacks exist, you'd have to be a right numpty no to prefer the ones you know aboot.'

King's usually attractive features were turning all sorts of shades of purple. 'What is this drawback, then?'

'My omniscience has almost no limits,' said the mirror, 'however, some-times a cloaking spell can prove a barrier. The home of the Freaks, whose hospitality your elusive rival is enjoying, is shrouded in some very powerful cloaking magic, which prevents any from finding it who do not seek it for the "right" reasons. It will take me some time to break through.'

'Magic, you say?' King stroked his chin. 'Oh, I think I can see the chubby little fingerprints of my dear Jillipoos all over this!'

'Very astute, Mr King,' confirmed the mirror. 'Indeed, the McCinder wimp left your workplace with every intention of carrying out your wishes, but bottled it at the last. She was dazed, confused and friendless, so she turned to the only person she could think of for support; namely the spher-ical Ms Cameron. Unfortunately, from our point of view, she could not have picked a more . . . heavyweight ally. Your Jillipoos now knows exactly what you're up to, and why.'

King nodded with sudden understanding. 'Nae wonder she was so keen to separate us.'

'Indeed,' said the mirror, 'and since she would, given the chance, almost certainly destroy me – which is not much more in your interest than mine – I trust you can assure me it's no gonnae happen?'

King grinned slyly. 'Oh, I'll keep you as lang as you're useful to me. So . . . how long before you've took doon that cloaking spell?'

'Hard to say, but rest assured I can. Patience, Mr King, is a virtue.'

'Aye,' said King. 'And I have virtue-ly nane.'

'Very droll,' said the mirror. 'You know . . . for the impatient man, there is a solution which would simplify matters and save considerable time.'

'Tell me more.'

'Well, I am wise to the ways of magic, and know that it is a very rare spell indeed that can outlive the magician who cast it. So if you get rid of the blob, your problems vanish.'

With a hellish roar, King wrenched the mirror from the wall and gripped it threateningly. 'Let's get one thing straight,' he snarled. 'Whatever happens, Jill will not be harmed on account of it. Clear?'

'Crystal, Mr King.'

'And you will on no account refer to her as "the blob".'

'As you wish, Mr King,' said the mirror, calm as ever. 'Is there some term you would prefer? The blimp? The hippo? The Stay-Puft Marshmallow Woman?'

'Avoid referring to her at all,' insisted King, replacing the mirror none too gently. 'You are on very dangerous ground.'

'No I'm not,' the mirror informed him matter-of-factly. 'If you destroy me, you lose all hope of destroying Snowy White. If you do so because I insulted your obnoxious, meddling, fat ex-girlfriend who is trying to thwart you, won't you feel a wee bit silly?'

King snarled.

'I know it is difficult for you humans to let go of that kind of feelings,' the mirror told him gently, 'but you do yourself no service by clinging to them. She – Jill – is actively plotting to thwart you. She wants to get between you and your ambitions. She wants to get between you and your right – your *right* – to be the bonniest man in Glasgow; the bonniest man anywhere. She is your enemy.'

'Aye,' said King. 'I suppose you're right.'

'I'm always right,' said the mirror. 'You have no friends apart from me.'

Always the professional, King gave the camera no hint that he was at all upset that day.

'Hello, and welcome to *The Reggie King Show*.

'Should Scots be given more rights to defend their homes? Later, I'll be talking to the wife and young son of a bear who was jailed after eating an intruder, who will be calling for a change in the law.

'But first . . . I'm sure my next guest needs no introduction. A young lad of only seventeen, he has already achieved great things for club and country. Who can forget that goal against England, eh? Please welcome . . . Harry Charmaine!'

The studio audience gave the footballer a thunderous cheer, which made him shrink awkwardly and slump shyly into his seat. He shook King's hand with no conviction at all.

'Harry, it's an honour to have you on the show. I don't mind telling you . . . I'm a huge fan.'

'Aye. Likewise.' Charmaine nodded vigorously.

'Now, whatever you do next, wherever your career takes you, let's be honest . . . you will probably always be remembered for one goal. Last year, at the tender age of sixteen, you became the youngest Scottish player ever to score against the Auld Enemy, England, in a full international. We've all seen it a hundred times before . . . but we all want to see it again, don't we?'

There was a roar of assent from the studio audience, who got to see on a giant screen what viewers could see on their TV screens: a golden moment of football action.

'Talk us through this, would you, Harry?' said King.

On-screen, an English defender was dispossessed by a Scottish midfielder, who stroked the ball with infinite elegance into the path of the onrushing Harry Charmaine, whose look of grim-faced, warrior-like confidence seemed to have nothing to do with the nervous wreck sitting opposite King in the studio. He controlled the ball easily with his chest, caught it with his laces on the volley, and it sailed from twenty yards into the back of the net.

This action was set to Charmaine's commentary: 'Well, it just . . . fell nicely for me, and I just blootered it. And sometimes when ye just blooter it, it goes in, and that's what happened on this occasion.'

'Fantastic,' said King. 'How does it make you feel to have achieved such a thing at such a young age?'

'Och, well,' shrugged Charmaine. 'Ye can only dae yer best, can't ye? Sometimes yer best is a memorable goal, and in that respect, I've been very fortunate.'

'Your humility is admirable. You're an inspiration.'

Charmaine blushed.

'Let's talk for a minute about this charity ball you've organised.'

'Okay,' said Charmaine.

'Now, last year's Scotland against Sectarianism concert was also your brainchild, so you are developing a reputation for being full of ideas . . . perhaps surprisingly so.'

'Aye, well,' shrugged Charmaine, shifting uncomfortably in his seat. 'Everybody's got good ideas, but when I get them, they actually happen, 'cause of who I am.'

'So tell us a bit more about this ball.'

'Well, it's gonnae take place in the Thistle Hotel, on the 18th, in just over two weeks' time, and the way ye get tickets is by entering the prize draw. That costs a fiver, so anyone can have a chance of going. Ye get a five-course meal, there's dancing, live music, and it'll be a' pure celebrities and that. Folk like . . . um . . . '

King cleared his throat. 'Well, *me* for a start!'

'Aye. Aye, yerself as well, of course. It'll be great. Anyone can go if they get a winning ticket, as I say. And all proceeds go to charity.'

'I'm sure the ladies will think it worth a fiver for the chance to dance with one or both of us, eh, Harry? What do you think, girls?'

The women in the studio audience screamed.

'I think that's a yes! So if you haven't entered the prize draw, what are you waiting for? The number's on your screen right now!'

Watching the interview in stolen glances (whilst polishing her foster family's entire collection of shoes) was Ella McCinder, who had already entered the draw as many times as her pocket money would allow.

She was trying not to make little noises in appreciation of Harry Charmaine's existence, as she usually did when he was on TV, since reminding her foster family that she existed was never a good idea.

'Oh, I do want to go to the ball,' said Kara.

'Me too,' said Clara.

'And me,' whispered Ella, regretting it as soon as she did.

'Shut up, you horrible girl!' hissed Clara.

'Fancy *that* going to the ball?' said Kara. 'What an embarrassment! The very idea!'

'The thought is making me sick!' cried Clara.

'Please don't upset my daughters,' their father said from behind his newspaper.

'Daddikins,' said Kara, slyly, slinking over and resting her chin on the arm of his chair like a dog. 'You know, as soon as the prize draw ends, there will be tickets popping up all over eBay. They wouldn't cost you more than a thousand pounds each, and it would mean ever so much to Clara and myself if we could go.'

'Ever so much,' echoed Clara, doing the same with the other arm.

Their dad cast his paper aside and put an arm round each of them. 'Well, why not? Nothing's too good for my wee girls!'

Ella felt like she was going to throw up. She finished the shoe she was working on, set it aside as quietly as she could, crept upstairs and locked herself in the bathroom.

Tears poured down her face as she looked in the mirror and said, 'Oh, I wish I could go to the ball! I wish, I wish, I wish I could go to the ball!'

Suddenly, she was blown over sideways by a great gust of wind.

A mini-tornado of sparkling blue dust appeared in the middle of the bathroom floor. It took form, into a kind-faced, middle-aged woman in a flowing, blue dress, with the back cut out for two tiny wings to poke through.

Ella gasped in terror.

The woman smiled warmly and said, 'Don't you be fear't o' me, Hen. I'm just yer Fairy Godmaw!'

[44]

CHAPTER 5

Scarlet Hood, known to her friends as Wee Red Hoodie (both for her name and for her preference for wearing just that), lived in fear of her granny.

'Ye've been fighting again,' said Granny, leaning forward dangerously on her rocking chair.

Wee Red turned her head to try to hide her black eye inside the red hood. She wanted to gloat. She wanted to boast of the mess she had made of the other girl's face, but fearless as the eleven-year-old was on the streets, she was reduced to a cowering rodent before her gran.

'Answer me when I talk to ye!' screamed Granny, picking up her walking stick. 'Have you been fighting?'

'Naw, I havenae!'

Granny hit her on the head with her walking stick. 'Don't you lie to me!' she screamed. She hit her on the head again. 'Don't you speak slang to me!' She hit her a third time. 'And get that hood doon when ye're talking to me! Show some respect, girl!'

In a rare moment of bravery, Wee Red took down her hood, squared up to her gran and said, 'How come it's awright for you to talk pure Scottish, but no me?'

'Speak up!' Granny yelled. 'You know fine well my hearing aid's near knackered!' She swung her walking stick once more, but Red side-stepped the blow.

Granny, in a well-practised move, flung herself onto the floor and writhed around as if bucking for a penalty.

'Oh, my hip!' said the old woman. 'My wee prosthetic hip! Oh, my heart! You're trying to kill me! Imagine sending me, just a wee auld woman, fleeing across the room like that! Help me up.'

Reluctantly, Wee Red guided her granny back into her rocking chair, to a chorus of 'Oh, my back! Oh, my knees! I hope I've no broken anything!' and got a slap across her face for her trouble.

'I know what you want! You want me deid! You want me oot the way so's ye can go and live on the streets! You're an ungrateful wee brat! I didnae have to take you in when yer maw and da' got themselves killed! You're evil, that's what you are. You're just born bad!'

She struck her granddaughter on the head once more for good measure.

Such was the life of Wee Red Hoodie.

'My . . . Fairy . . . Godmaw?'

Though the limits of Ella's belief had been tested a lot lately, this . . . this was something else.

'Aye, deary. Let me explain,' said the Fairy Godmaw with a soft, kind voice. 'There's many ways ye can have a wish come true. Ye can get the big hauf o' a wishbone. Ye can fling a penny doon a well. Ye can see a falling star. Ye can blow oot the candles on a birthday cake. Or ye can make up yer ain wee ritual . . . it really doesnae make much difference, but those things don't always work. There has to be magic in the air, or the planets have to be aligned just right. Something like that.

'Noo, if you happen to be lucky enough to have a Fairy Godmother . . . and if she hears yer wish . . . that's wan way to guarantee yer wish will be granted.'

Ella nodded slowly, pulling herself up from the floor and sitting on the toilet seat. She had reached the point where acceptance of the impossible was growing on her quite rapidly. 'So . . . how did I come to have a Fairy Godmother?'

'Well, you know there is magic in the world, and magic breeds magic, so when you've been in contact wi' someone magical, it rubs aff on ye, and you shouldnae be surprised when magic starts finding you.'

Ella nodded slowly. 'So, like, when I talked to Jill, she left a magical residue on me or that, and it's enough to pluck you oot the faerie realm and attract you to me like a magnet . . . or something?'

'Well, actually she called me on her mobile,' said the Fairy Godmaw. 'Anyway, I'm here to make your fondest wish come true.' With that, she produced a ticket for Harry Charmaine's charity ball and handed it to Ella. 'Now, don't you lose that!'

Ella knew it was a bit rude, but she couldn't restrain herself from examining the winning hologram on the ticket.

She threw her arms around her Fairy Godmaw, squealing, 'How can I ever thank you?'

'That'll dae fine,' said her Fairy Godmaw, smiling kindly.

'Oh, but . . . oh . . .' Ella could scarcely grasp the reality of it all. 'I don't have anything to wear!'

'Don't you mind that, it'll sort itself when the time comes. Your clothes will be transformed. You'll be transformed! Ye'll no recognise yersel'!'

'But . . .' a horrible thought struck Ella. 'Reggie King will be there. I don't think I'm his favourite person . . .'

Her Fairy Godmaw shook her head. 'Don't you worry aboot that. He'll no recognise you. Your foster sisters won't recognise you. Naebody who's looked at you and seen anything but the wonderful young lady you are will recognise you. Kara and Clara only see a skivvy. King only saw a little girl he could use to his ain ends. They've never seen the real you and they're no interested in the real you. But that's who's gonnae be shining through at the ball.'

Ella grinned and cried at the same time. 'Just like a fairytale.'

'Something like that,' her Fairy Godmaw agreed. 'Now . . . to business. Is there a pumpkin or anything in the house?'

'I think there's usually some courgettes.'

'That'll dae. Put wan oot in the driveway when it's time to go. It'll turn into a big pink limo for ye.'

'Okay,' said Ella, not fully understanding.

'The most important thing . . . whatever happens at the ball, you must be oot o' there by midnight.'

She hugged Ella tightly. 'Good luck, my dear. May all yer flowers have an odd number of petals!'

And with a puff of sparkling blue smoke, she was gone as suddenly as she had appeared.

'We grow oor ain vegetables, here,' said Crabbit, handing Snowy a trowel. 'Once in a blue moon, Jill's Fairy Godmaw shows up wi' some bags o' shopping, but for the most part, ye don't dig, ye don't eat.'

'Happy to pull my weight,' said Snowy.

'Good lad.'

Snowy and the Freaks shuffled out into the garden. There was a slight shimmering in the distance, as though they were surrounded by a thin layer of running water.

'See that?' said Crabbit, pointing to the shimmering. 'That's the limit of the cloaking spell that's keeping you alive. Ye can step outside it if ye like, but yer mate will spot ye nae bother wi' his magic mirror, so I wouldnae.'

Snowy and the Freaks busied themselves with the gardening, and collecting wood for the fire. Aside from the occasional murmur of 'Bob the Builder' and subsequent giggling, there was no conversation between the six of them.

That night, Snowy was curled on the sofa, gazing into the blazing fire, enjoying the patterns it was making, and the gentle warmth upon his face.

The fire in front of him was a pale reflection of the fire in his heart.

The woman who had burst so unexpectedly into his life had told him he was in mortal danger, then ripped him out of reality as he knew it . . . and utterly, utterly, stolen his heart in the process.

He heaved a heavy sigh. He didn't know when or if he would ever see her again. That bothered him much more than being in mortal danger.

'Haw, Snowy!' called Crabbit from upstairs. 'You awake?'

'Yes, Crabbit,' Snowy sighed sleepily. 'What is it?'

'Get yersel' up here,' called Crabbit.

Snowy yawned, grumbled, then climbed the creaky wooden stairs to the much colder bedroom of the Freaks.

'Sometimes we tell each other stories at night,' Crabbit explained. 'Keeps us all a bit less miserable and helps Nono get to sleep.'

'Nonononono!' Nono agreed.

'We was wondering,' Crabbit went on, 'if you'd like to be our storyteller tonight?'

'Oh, I . . . I've never been much of a storyteller,' said Snowy.

'Story now,' insisted Dagger, bearing his teeth.

'Well,' said Snowy, straining to think. 'I do know one story about a handsome young man from the Highlands. At least, I have heard it said that he is handsome, but I couldn't say.

'He had always wanted to move to the big city, so when his great uncle in Glasgow passed away and left him his flat, the young man was ready to start his new life.

'He hoped his life in Glasgow would bring him a job, a woman, and with any luck, some adventure.

'Well, of those three things, fate chose to give him two . . . or rather, give him one and show him the briefest, most wonderful, most agonising glimpse of another.

'For you see, his life became an adventure when she came into it. She was like a goddess!

'She knocked on his door and he had no sooner opened it than he was quite mad with his love for her. He had never believed in love at first sight until that moment.

'Even when she warned him he was in terrible danger, he could think only of her beauty and how his heart ached with love for her. Even when she made a refugee of him, whisking him away to a strange place full of strange – ers . . . he could only think of her. She was his world: nothing else mattered . . . which is just as well, because everything else that was his was taken away. But he didn't know if or when he would ever see her again.'

Snowy was silent for a long moment. He felt better for having spoken these words aloud. They hadn't sounded nearly as ridiculous as he had thought they would.

'What happened next?' asked Glaikit.

'I don't know how this story ends. It isn't finished yet.'

'Aww!' cried Glaikit. 'But I wanna hear the end now!'

Crabbit smiled wryly. 'I think our friend Snowy might be talking about himsel'.'

Snowy nodded slowly in the dim lamplight.

'Well, I'll tell ye this . . . ye could dae a lot worse than oor Jill,' Crabbit informed him. 'Of course, if you hurt her, we'll rip oot yer liver.'

Another long silence filled the room, before Glaikit began chuckling unaccountably.

'What are you laughing at?' demanded Crabbit.

'Bob the Builder,' Glaikit recounted, and the Freaks burst into hysterical laughter.

'Nonononononononononono!' laughed Nono, his head spinning so fast that it became entangled in his bedclothes. A muffled, panicky 'Nonononononononono!' could be heard from the great lump of sheet and blanket that had replaced his head.

'Och, don't make Nono laugh in bed,' Crabbit snapped, dragging herself out of bed and untangling him. 'He'll strangle himsel'!'

Snowy gave an embarrassed chuckle. 'Well . . . goodnight, everyone.'

He climbed carefully downstairs and into bed, relieved to be in the warmth of the roaring fire once more.

He still couldn't get his head around how funny the Freaks had found that 'Bob the Builder' remark. It really hadn't been that funny.

Then it occurred to him that that was probably the first time a non-Freak had cracked a joke in their house. Were they so used to each other – or tired of each other – that they couldn't make each other laugh? Maybe laughter wasn't important to their relationship with each other.

Snowy tried to put himself in their shoes for a minute, and realised how lonely their existence must be.

It wasn't the joke itself that had provoked such uproarious laughter, it was the fact that he had shared it with them. That really meant something to them.

Snowy suddenly felt very close to the Freaks.

Who would have thought? With one lame, half-hearted attempt at wit, he had become family.

Jack took a deep breath as he opened his front door, knowing what he would see. The imposing (if short) figure of his mother was framed in the doorway, glaring angrily.

She was a stout woman with greying hair, nicotine-stained omelettes hanging around her eyes, cheeks that looked a lot like a dog's floppy ears, and great boulders of flesh hanging over her flabby, folded arms.

'What time d'ye call this?' she growled. 'I just sent ye for messages.'

Jack dumped his shopping bags by the door, then squeezed his way past his unmoving mother, stepping over empty beer bottles and half-full bin bags to get to the living room.

A stranger in the living room would have remarked upon the mess. Jack barely noticed the Union Flag, once hung proudly over the mantelpiece, now dangled limply from a single nail.

'I was at Jill's,' Jack informed his mother.

'Oh,' she grunted, and sagged into the sofa.

'How's your day been?' Jack asked.

'Am I no getting a cup o' tea?' asked his mum. 'I've no had wan a' day!'

'Well, if all else fails, you could aye try getting it yersel'.'

'Oh, that's just great, that is!' his mother spat. 'That attitude's just fantastic, so it is! See you? You've got less respect for me every time I talk to ye. That's yer sister's influence, that is!'

Jack harrumphed and made tea for his mum, coffee for himself.

'Speaking o' Jill . . .' said Jack.

'Och, don't start.'

'How'd ye no just talk to her?'

She said nothing.

'She misses you, you know.'

'Aye, well . . . that's no what she said last time I seen her.'

Jack sighed. 'That was four years ago, Maw.'

His mother harrumphed.

'She'd really like to get back in touch.'

'She knows where I am if she wants to apologise.'

'Yous two are as bad as each other,' said Jack. 'Can ye no just let bygones be bygones? She's got a new job now.'

'Aye, well, that's mair than I can say for you!'

'Just thought you'd like to know how she was getting on.'

'She can aye phone me hersel' and tell me.'

'Aye, and you can phone her, too. Bear in mind you can be a very intimidating person, Mum. And she knows you don't approve of her lifestyle.'

' "Lifestyle"? Is that what ye call it? I call it turning her back on Christ.'

Jack rolled his eyes. 'Och, don't give us yer "Christ" patter. When was the last time you actually went to church? And by "church", I don't mean Ibrox.'

His mother folded her fleshy face into a frown. 'Aye, but that's no the point, is it? I mean, see a' that . . . stuff she's doing? A' that magic and that? I mean, it's no right, is it?' She paused. 'And where's my swallae?'

'Erm . . . me and Jill were chatting and lost track o' time a bit. It was after ten afore I got tae the supermarket.' He shrugged. 'Sorry.'

'Och, that's just great, that is! You and that sister of yours!'

'Look, I didnae mean it to happen,' said Jack. 'It just sort of happened. She's going through a lot the noo.'

Maw harrumphed.

'I'll nip tae the shops again the morra, awright?'

'Aye. What I'm I gonnae dae the night, but?'

'You could try staying sober for wan night,' muttered Jack.

'Well thanks for nothing.' Maw sipped her tea, and resigned herself to changing the subject. 'Anyways, ye missed a' the excitement earlier.'

'Oh, aye?' said Jack.

'Aye, ye know that asylum seeker that lives two flairs up?'

Jack's heart was suddenly in his throat. 'Aye?'

'Immigration came for her and took her away. There was a whole big hoo-ha. Jack? Jack . . . ? Where are ye going?'

Jack was feeling sick when he reached Rapunzel's front door. His heart was pounding, his stomach was turning, and the back of his throat was burning.

The door was boarded up.

Jack pounded the chipboard until his fists bled and let out a roar of anguish.

'What's the matter wi' you?' his mother asked, following far behind up the stairs. 'What? Did ye know her or that?'

'I know her,' said Jack. 'I . . . love her.'

His mother roared with laughter. 'Oh, aye, looks like she seen you coming all right.'

'You know nothing!' screamed Jack. 'Nothing!'

'I know enough to know what these people are like. She doesnae belang in this country. And if we don't have some rules to keep them oot, there'll end up mair o' them than there are of us!'

'You're nothing but a spiteful, poison-minded bigot,' spat Jack. 'You're not my mother, and I'm not staying in your hoose another day.'

The bus that carried Jack over the Squinty Bridge also carried him over a very strange plant that was growing out of the River Clyde; a plant the like of which had never been seen by mortal eyes.

It grew and grew and grew, and had soon pushed its way right through the Squinty Bridge, which the police had consequently closed.

An onlooker was heard to remark, 'Christ! They're just after getting the thing fixed!'

CHAPTER 6

The Wolf approached his target stealthily; a quaint little brick house that, if he had his way, would soon be rubble.

He knocked on the door, grinning nastily with the delicious sensation of impending victory.

'Aye, who is it?' came a voice from within.

'Why, it is your old friend, the Big, Bad Wolf. Little pigs, won't you please let me in?'

'Sod off!' replied three pigs in unison.

'How rude,' chuckled the Wolf. 'I'm afraid I shall have to huff, and puff, and blow your house down.'

Percy and Peter huddled close in fear, whilst their elder brother, Paddy, smiled confidently. 'On ye go, then,' he called to the wolf outside.

'Careful, Paddy,' said Percy. 'He really knows how to huff and puff.'

'He's right,' insisted Peter. 'He got Percy's straw hoose and my stick hoose. Let's get oot the back door and run for it while we still can.'

'Haud yer horses,' Paddy insisted calmly. 'See, my hoose is a brick hoose, wi' double glazing and a top-of-the-range security system. And I'm telling you, that wolf can huff and puff all he wants. This hoose will stand longer than him. I guarantee it.'

They had not long to wait to find out.

They heard the Wolf huff.

They heard the Wolf puff.

They heard the Wolf's gale-force breath buffeting the sturdy brick walls of the house.

And then . . . nothing.

The pigs laughed while the Wolf struggled to get his breath back.

'Haw, Wolfie!' cried Paddy. 'Blow harder!'

His brothers fell on their backs, kicking the air with all their trotters, helpless with laughter.

Again the Wolf huffed.

Again the Wolf puffed.

Again the brick house stood its ground.

'My granny can blow harder!' yelled Paddy Pig. 'Gie up smoking, then come back!'

For the third time, the Wolf huffed.

For a third time, the Wolf puffed.

For a third time, his efforts came to nothing.

'This is your final warning, pigs,' panted the wolf. 'I do not take kindly to defiance. Less so, mocking.'

'Ye've come to the wrang place, then!' jeered Paddy.

'I would not be so complacent in your position,' growled the Wolf, the gentle, velvety quality of his voice now gone. 'Your house may be strong, but wolfish cunning will be your undoing.'

The pigs grunted and wheezed with maniacal porcine mirth.

They laughed until Paddy hissed, 'Ssh!'

The pigs were silent.

'You hear that?'

Indeed, they could hear something. They could hear the unmistakable sound of someone – or something – climbing the brick walls of their house.

'He's no gonnae try and climb down the chimney, is he?' breathed Peter.

Paddy grinned. 'Oh, boy, this is gonnae be good.' He spun to face his brothers, his features suddenly serious. 'Go down to the cellar and bring me my mud-warmer.'

'Yer . . . ?'

'What?' asked Peter and Percy, one word each.

'You know,' the eldest pig insisted impatiently. 'The really big pot. I've been using it to warm mud on the fire.'

'That's no a bad idea, that,' Percy mused.

'I've just been using the kettle,' shrugged Peter.

'Go!' yelled Paddy. 'There isnae much time!'

Peter and Percy scattered, while Paddy started a fire.

'Oh, but I am clever,' the Wolf commended himself, as he reached the roof. 'Let it be known that none shall mock the Big, Bad Wolf and live to tell of it.'

He dived head-first down the chimney, relishing the thought of the terror-stricken looks on the pigs' faces as they realised that his teeth would be the last thing they ever saw . . .

That thought left his mind with a SPLASH!

Suddenly he was in a large pot of boiling water.

Suddenly he was in unspeakable agony all over.

Suddenly he was being cooked alive, in darkness, for the pigs were holding the lid on the pot.

There was no escape for the Wolf, except, perchance, the mercy of the pigs.

'Please!' he cried, closing his eyes against the possibility that the boiling water would cook away his sight forever. 'Let me out.'

'Only if you promise to be good,' came the mocking voice of one of the pigs.

'Oh, yes,' yelled the Wolf, as bits of his fur came away from his flesh. 'Super good! You won't recognise me.'

The pigs lifted the pot lid, and out slunk the Wolf, the worse for wear with red patches of scalded flesh showing where his once-magnificent fur had fallen away. He wanted nothing more than to destroy the pigs there and then, but was too weak to do anything of the sort.

'Ye'll have had yer tea,' Paddy Pig jeered, as the poor, defeated creature slithered out the front door.

He bathed himself in a nearby puddle, trying to cool his burns as he listened to the pigs celebrating.

He was too weak to get far enough away to escape the rowdy singing:

> If ye're proud to be a grumphie clap yer trotters!
> If ye're proud to be a grumphie clap yer trotters!
> If ye're proud to be a grumphie,
> Proud to be a grumphie,
> If ye're proud to be a grumphie clap yer trotters!

Then, silencing the others, came the unmistakable voice of Paddy, more roaring than singing:

> Ye can stick yer wolfish cunning 'neath yer tail!
> If ye try to blow oor hoose doon you will fail!
> Naw, we don't care where ye come fae,
> You will never beat a grumphie,
> Ye can stick yer wolfish cunning 'neath yer tail!

All three pigs roared with laughter as the Wolf muttered, 'Oh, you may have survived my wolfish cunning . . . let's see how you cope with wolfish wrath.'

Then he slithered into the shadows to a chorus of 'Stand up if ya hate the Wolf'.

Jack had a finger in one ear to drown out the whirring of Jill's printer. To his other ear, he pressed Jill's mobile.

'Look, I know things look bad at the moment, darling . . . Aye, you keep the chin up, okay? I dunno what else to say. Upenda will be fine, she will. She's a tough wee cookie . . . What? . . . Rumpole who? . . . Okay, sweetheart . . . Love you too. Bye.'

Jack let out a roar of anger and threw the mobile down on the sofa.

'Oi!' said Jill. 'Watch it wi' that.'

'Sorry,' said Jack, over the humming and buzzing of the printer.

'Are you okay?'

'I'm fine,' said Jack. 'I'm no the one who's been locked up and had my wean taken away!'

Rapunzel, Jack had found out, was in Dungavel – a detention centre for failed asylum seekers some thirty miles from Glasgow.

'You'll never guess where Upenda is. She's wi' the same foster family that's ruining Ella's life. I didnae tell Punzy how rotten they are, of course.'

Jill sighed. 'I'll send Ella a text saying look after her as much as possible. She'll be alright. If there's anyone we can count on, it's oor Ella.'

Jack sprawled back on a beanbag and rubbed his eyes. 'I'm so tired.'

'You should lie doon for a bit,' said Jill. 'Then you should phone Maw.'

Jack harrumphed.

'I'm sure she'll have calmed doon a bit by noo.'

'She might have, but I havenae,' growled Jack. 'I'm no phoning her.'

'I wouldnae like to see yous pair drifting apart.'

'Says the one who hasnae spoken to her for four years.'

'Exactly,' said Jill, sitting on the arm of the sofa and clasping her hands thoughtfully. 'That's how I know ... it's easier to close the door than open it. Don't make the same mistake I made.'

Jack grunted, then sighed. 'How can they just lock up people who havenae done anything wrang? How can they send people back to places they know fine are dangerous? And Upenda ... Upenda's lived in Glasgow almost all her life! She's got the accent and everything. How can they do this to people?'

'Too many folk like Maw in the world to stop them,' Jill shrugged. 'Folk that believe what they read in the papers.'

'She's really upset,' said Jack. 'I'm worried aboot her. She wasnae making any sense. Kept saying Upenda's in danger ... gibbering on aboot Rumpole somebody or other ...'

'I thought she had an appeal pending, anyway?'

'Lawyer's on holiday,' said Jack. 'That's how the Home Office thinks they can get away wi' it. They're probably right.'

'That's some amount of ink you're using,' Jill remarked. 'What are you printing anyway?'

Jack leapt up like a shot and tried to get between Jill and the printer. Alas, it takes longer to get up out of a beanbag than to slide off the arm of a sofa.

'Jack . . . why are you printing oot pictures o' Dungavel?' She picked up several printouts and examined them. 'From . . . all different angles?'

'I was . . . thinking o' visiting her, see?' said Jack, swallowing hard. 'I'd like to know what it looks like afore I go. So's . . . so's it doesnae take me by surprise.'

He blushed furiously. It was a chocolate-faced toddler lie, and he knew it.

'Jack . . . knock knock?'

'Who's there?'

'Giraffe.'

'Giraffe who?'

'Giraffe yer heid!' cried Jill. 'You're planning to bust her oot, aren't ye?'

'If I was . . .' said Jack, carefully, 'You'd be right behind me all the way, right?'

'Aw, naw,' said Jill. 'You can be stupid enough for the pair of us.'

'But it's an emergency, Jill. She's gonnae get deported! I might . . .' he swallowed hard, fighting back tears. 'I might never see her again.'

'I'm on your side, Jack,' said Jill. 'I'm just saying . . . there's mair than one way to fight. Have you no heard the saying: the pen is mightier than the sword?'

Jack rubbed his eyes and yawned. 'So, like . . . if I was to challenge you to a duel, right? And I says, "Choose your weapon", right? And there's a claymore and a biro . . . you're telling me you'd go for the pen? Dae yersel' a favour, Jill . . . don't take up duelling.'

'Stop trying to be clever, Jack. It doesnae suit ye,' snapped Jill. 'What I'm trying to say is ye can write, fax, email MPs, MSPs, MEPs, councillors, newspapers . . . ye can join campaigns, stage peaceful protests, organise petitions. Naebody was ever jailed for possession of a pen.'

'That's your way,' grumbled Jack. 'Nae offence, but your way's got "too little, too late" written all over it.'

'You don't need to be an action hero to prove you love her, Jack.'

Jack laughed out loud. 'Is that what you think? That this is aboot me?'

'I think there's a bit of a daydreamer in you, Jack, and I think there's a better way to go about this.'

'I cannae leave her to her fate, Jill. But we won't be on the run forever. All I need to do is keep her oot harm's way until her lawyer gets back. She's got a really good case, if it ever gets heard.'

'Tell me what your brilliant plan is,' said Jill, resigning herself to hearing him out. 'At least I might be able to . . . improve it a little.'

'You'll try and talk me out of it,' Jack informed her huffily, crossing his arms.

'Probably,' said Jill. 'But if you're that determined, I'll never be able to, so why are you feart?'

Jack shrugged.

'Okay, Punzy is here . . .' He picked up a picture of Dungavel (which looked a lot like a fairytale castle, with towers and turrets) and drew a circle round an upstairs window. 'The first thing I need to do is blow a hole in the fence.'

'Blow a hole in it?'

'Aye, blow a hole in it. Hear me out.'

'Wi', like, explosives and that?'

'Aye!'

Jill rolled her eyes. 'Jack, that can't possibly work.'

'Ye said ye'd hear me out,' said Jack.

'Sorry.'

'The explosion is just a distraction, see? It'll happen at the other side of the building. Then I fly in from a nearby tree wi' a hang-glider . . .'

'A hang-glider?'

'Aye! A hang-glider! That's you interrupting again.'

'Sorry.'

'Then I throw a wee stone at her windae, and I call, quietly but urgently, "Haw! Punzy! Chuck us yer hair!" That's the brilliant part. See, her hair's that long it would easily stretch fae that windae to the ground when she lets it doon. Then I just climb up her hair and run off wi' her.'

Jill was speechless.

Jack crossed his arms, looking slightly hurt. 'You don't like it, do you?'

'I think it's very, um . . . creative.'

Jack snorted.

'If you don't mind a wee bit of constructive criticism . . .'

'Go on?'

Jill sighed. 'Okay, in the first place, once you bring explosives into this, you cross the line between a wee crime and a big crime. Don't be so stupid.'

'That's constructive?'

'In the second place, where are you getting these explosives?'

Jack shifted uncomfortably. The thoughts he was expressing sounded a lot better in his head. He was beginning to realise that when he spoke them aloud, they became a bit silly. 'Well . . . I read in the paper that there's army bases all over Scotland where they try oot bombs and that . . .'

'Jack, has it occurred to you that it's a lot easier to break a detainee oot o' Dungavel than it is to steal weapons from the military?'

'Aha!' said Jack, jabbing a finger at her in triumph. 'Then you admit it's possible!'

Jill rubbed the bridge of her nose. 'Okay, I think this is stupidity limitation. Suppose, just suppose, I agreed to help you get together a slightly less hare-brained scheme . . . would you agree to leave bombs and hang-gliders out of it?'

'Oh!' cried Jack, leaping to his feet and pacing like a caged panther. 'Oh, I've got it! New plan! Right, this one's a beauty.'

'I'm listening.'

'Right, instead of using bombs . . . I'll set fire to the place!'

'What?'

'They'll evacuate and gather at their fire assembly point . . . and then all I have to do is bungee jump out of a nearby tree, grab Punzy just before I go BOING! And we're away!'

Jill stared at him incredulously. 'I seriously think you've lost the ability to think like an adult.'

'Well,' said Jack, with a nasty sneer, still pacing. 'Pardon me if I'm no thinking quite as clearly as Little Miss I'm-So-Much-More-Intelligent-And-Mature-Than-My-Stupid-Baby-Brother-Except-When-I'm-Defenestrating-My-Ex-Boyfriend's-Stuff . . .' he needed a deep breath to continue after that mouthful. 'It's only because the woman I love has been abducted and locked up, and I'm worried that if she gets deported she's gonnae get killed.'

Jill knew her brother well enough to know what was coming next. 'Please don't punch the wall . . .'

Jack punched the wall. Then sat down, trying to nurse his knuckles whilst not letting on it hurt.

'I shouldnae have flung Reggie's stuff oot,' said Jill. 'You were right to try and stop me. So I know that being upset makes you dae stupid things that you'll regret later. Can you wiggle your fingers?'

Jack satisfied her that he hadn't broken any bones.

'Do you want some ice?'

'Naw. It's kinda nice to hurt on the outside.'

Jill gave him a small smile. 'Look, do you want to hear my plan?'

'Go on then.'

'Bear in mind, I'd really rather you didnae follow through with this at all, but if you insist, I'd rather you did it . . . well, a wee bit sanely.'

'Aye,' said Jack. 'Go on.'

She clapped him on the knee and twitched her nose at him. 'Just this once, I'm gonnae let you use something from my Special Cupboard.'

'Now we're talking,' said Jack.

Jill left the living room and returned presently with something in her hands. Jack strained his neck trying to peek.

Jill sat down next to him and revealed a small snow globe with an old-fashioned clock in the middle.

'See this?' she said. 'This is the most powerful magical object in my collection. In fact, it might just be one of the most powerful magical objects in the world. There's only one of these and you can only ever use it the once.'

'What's it do?' asked Jack, annoyed now, for he had the definite feeling she was teasing him.

'If you break it . . . for a few minutes, it stops time.'

'Just a few minutes?'

'Aye.'

Jack nodded slowly. 'Should be enough time for me to blow a hole in the fence and get in.'

Jill could barely contain herself from throwing the snow globe across the room in temper. 'Oh, for – Jack, would you give it a rest wi' this obsession of yours wi' blowing things up?'

'Do you have a better idea?'

'Noo ye mention it,' said Jill with an exasperated sigh, 'how d'ye no just wait until the main gate opens to let a delivery in, then stop time.'

Jack folded his arms and frowned, embarrassed slightly by the simplicity and explosionlessness of her plan. 'Aye . . . I suppose that could work.'

'Not as exciting as your plan,' chuckled Jill, 'but it might just come off.'

'How do I get her oot the building then, smarty pants? I mean, she'll be frozen too. If I'm no allowed to blow anything up, and I've only got a few minutes, I cannae see any way it could work . . .'

Jill shook her head. 'There's one thing that can unfreeze her.'

'What's that?'

'True love.'

Jack grinned. 'It's always true love wi' magic, isn't it? Well, don't worry, I've got bags o' that!'

'Aye, but does she?'

Jack fixed his sister with a deadly glare. 'Just what is that supposed to mean?'

'It means that when you call to her, she will unfreeze only if you love her absolutely, wi' all yer heart, and she feels the same aboot you.'

'She does.'

'Are you sure?' asked Jill, and braced herself as a beekeeper might before stirring up the bees.

Jack pointed a raging finger at her. 'You think she's just using me to stay in the country, don't you? You sound just like Maw.'

'That's unfair,' Jill told him calmly. 'Maw would say it like it's a bad thing. But if you're right, and she and her wean would be in grave danger if they got deported, she might think she's got nae choice. I think anyone'd dae the same.'

'Well, you're wrong.' Jack crossed his arms defensively. 'See when she looks me in the eye and tells me she loves me? I know she's no lying. I know it in my heart.'

'I hope you're right,' Jill said, softly.

'Well, I am right,' Jack insisted, sulkily. 'I am.'

'All the same, I want you to promise me . . .'

'Aye, what?'

'Promise me that if you call to her and she doesnae call back . . . you'll no just hang around and wait for the spell to run down. You'll get the hell out of there and no look back.'

'No gonnae happen,' Jack told her with grim resolve.

'What's the harm promising then?' Jill asked reasonably. 'Look, if you don't promise, you're no getting the snow globe.'

'Fine,' said Jack. 'I promise that if I call to her and she doesnae call back, I'm oot o' there quicker than you can say "Houdini".'

'Good.'

'But it's no gonnae happen.'

'I hope you're right,' said Jill. 'I really do. Anyway,' she felt the need to steer the conversation away from that awkward topic, 'how's she getting her hair doon to ye if she cannae open a windae?'

'The windaes dae open a crack. Look . . .' he shuffled through his print-outs until he found the one he was looking for. 'See this? This picture was taken at a protest a couple of years back. See how the asylum seekers are sticking their arms oot to wave at the protestors? I don't reckon they open much more than that. Unless, of course, you stick a car jack in and force it open.'

Jill grinned. 'Okay. I think we came up with a plan.'

'Aye. We're both brilliant. Especially me.'

Jill let that one slide. 'I think we need to unwind a bit. I'll get the coffees in: you see what's on telly.'

Jack put the TV on, to see the astonishing image of the biggest plant he had ever seen, growing out of the Squinty Bridge.

'The mysterious beanstalk,' a newsreader was saying, 'is growing so fast that it has caused severe structural damage to the Clyde Arc Bridge, known locally as the "Squinty Bridge".'

'No way!' breathed Jack.

'Disturbingly, a strange energy field is preventing anyone or anything from getting within a metre of the plant. Government ministers are anxious that the giant plant could become dangerous if it grows much bigger.'

Jack nodded slowly, understanding. 'I'm the only wan that can climb the beanstalk. I planted it.' He stroked his chin. 'It's my destiny.'

'Horticultural experts have as yet been unable to identify the plant, or shed any light on its possible origins.'

Jack heard Jill coming back through, and quickly turned the telly off. 'Nothing good on,' he said. She didn't need to know about this.

But Jack knew he would climb the beanstalk. He had to. He would go crazy not knowing what was up there, not knowing what the strange little drunk man had meant by all the strange things he had said.

Jack would climb the beanstalk.

But it had to wait until Rapunzel was free.

CHAPTER 7

'I'd like you all to meet Upenda,' said the social worker, holding the terrified youngster's hand. 'Upenda's going to be staying with you for a few days.'

'I'm absolutely delighted to meet you,' said Kara, with a horridly false smile.

'Delighted,' said Clara. 'Absolutely delighted.'

Ella's gaze fell upon the bronze-skinned child whose destiny was being ripped from her hands. She couldn't have been more than eight.

She knew what it was like to be that child . . . only a bit older and better able to cope. Certainly Ella knew what it was like to have one's life turned upside down many times in quick succession; to have everything one thought one knew about the world turn out to be wrong.

She had to protect this child, whatever the cost. So after the social worker left, she summoned all her courage and said, 'I want you guys to know, if you treat Upenda like you've treated me, I'm gonnae blow the whistle. I don't care what happens to me. Come on, Upenda, I'll show you your room.'

On the way upstairs, Ella got a text from Jill asking her to look out for the kid. She chuckled to herself and replied: *way ahed o u.*

Jack could hear his heart thundering so loudly in his ears that he wondered that the security guard positioned directly ahead of him couldn't hear it.

He was hiding up a tree, some hundred yards from the main gate of Dungavel, the cream-coloured castle.

He heard the distant sound of a van. Or was it the wind?

No, it was a mail van.

Coming closer.

His heart beat faster. He could see it now.

Jack felt sick.

A part of him wanted to abandon the whole scheme and just go home, but he knew there would be no way to live with himself if he didn't try. Not after coming this far.

The driver of the van spoke briefly to the guard, then the gates opened to let it through.

NOW! screamed a voice in Jack's head.

He leapt from the tree and ran forward, roaring as he did. No point hiding now!

The guard leapt into action ready to take him down.

Jack threw the snow globe on the ground.

A smash . . . and all was silence.

The startled security guard, stopped in time, had struck a hilarious pose, ready to tackle the maniac who was rushing him.

The dirt squirting upwards from the wheel of the mail van hung in mid-air.

A bird-dropping waited patiently, mere inches from the ground.

'It works!' cried Jack, tweaking the guard's nose, then dashing in.

'Rapunzel!' he called. 'Rapunzel!'

There was no response.

He remembered Jill's warning. He remembered his promise.

'Och, come on, Punzy! Don't do this to me!'

Into the silence that surrounded him, he yelled, *'RAPUNZEL!'*

A window opened just a few inches.

'Jack?' he heard her call back. 'Jack, is that you?'

Jack had never been happier to hear her beautiful, lilting, accented voice.

He was so overwhelmed with emotion, he didn't know whether to laugh or cry. But he knew he had no time for either.

'Rapunzel, chuck us yer hair. Try and catch it on something, so's it doesnae hurt when I climb up. Hurry.'

Down came her long rope of silky, black, pleated hair, all the way to the ground.

When Jack placed his hand upon it, it took him a moment to remember what he was there to do, for all he could think about was how much he had missed stroking it. It was as soft and as warm as he remembered it, and still smelled of apples.

With a sigh, Jack began his climb, clinging fast to the rope of hair as he planted boot in front of boot on the wall of the detention centre.

When he reached the window, he still had to hang on to the hair, for the window ledge was not wide enough for his feet.

'Hang on,' he breathed with a confidence he didn't feel. 'I'll have you oota here in a jiffy.'

'What about the guards?'

'I've stopped time,' said Jack, somehow managing to get the jack in place. He stuck an arm in the window space for purchase and began turning the handle. It was a tough job. The window was not designed to be easily budged but he felt more determined now than he had ever felt in his life.

'Stopped time how?' asked a bemused Rapunzel.

Jack flashed her a boyish grin as his muscles strained. 'I'm just . . . a hell of a guy.'

Finally he heard a crack and the window, slowly but surely, began to give way.

Rapunzel wasted no time in climbing out once she had enough space.

The kiss Jack had longed to make, the soft, succulent, kiss-to-end-all-kisses, was relegated to a peck on the cheek. For he knew he simply didn't have time to savour the moment.

'What now?' asked Rapunzel.

'Now,' said Jack, producing a pair of scissors, 'you get a haircut.'

'What?'

'Darling, it's the only way we can both climb down.'

'No way,' Rapunzel insisted flatly. 'My hair means a lot to me. I'm not leaving without every inch.'

'Women!' growled Jack with a roll of his eyes. 'What do you suggest? It's too high to jump.'

'Here,' said Rapunzel. She passed her hair behind the jack, which was still wedged in place. 'Hold onto me as tight as you can.'

Jack readily agreed.

Rapunzel grabbed the rope of hair on the other side of the jack and began slowly feeding it through, lowering them to the ground.

'Doesn't that hurt?' asked Jack.

'Yes,' Rapunzel replied. 'A lot.'

They landed safely and Rapunzel stuffed her hair into her jumper, making her look heavily pregnant – a look Jack thought she rather suited.

'Run,' Jack told her, as they made a run for the exit.

Rapunzel had to stop and look at the time-frozen guard.

'Punzy!' cried Jack. 'We don't have time!'

'I'm sorry, I just . . . I've never seen anyone frozen in time . . .'

'I know it's fascinating,' said Jack with a note of urgency in his voice, 'but we really must –'

'Why can we see?'

'What?'

'Time has stopped,' said Rapunzel. 'So everything moving must stop, including light. If light isn't moving, it can't hit the back of our eyes, so we should not be able to see.'

'I don't know –'

'And why are we not freezing to death?' Rapunzel asked. 'Heat is also a kind of light.'

'I don't entirely understand –'

'And why can we breathe? The tiny particles in the oxygen molecules shouldn't be moving, which means it can't have a chemical reaction with our bodies, which means we can't breathe.'

'I suppose I never really gave it much thought,' pondered Jack.

The bird dropping landed.

The van rolled forward.

The guard moved towards where Jack had been when he saw him last, then stopped and took a step back. From his point of view, Jack had suddenly changed position and conjured Rapunzel by his side.

Jack took advantage of his momentary confusion by punching him hard on the jaw.

'Ow!' said Jack, nursing his fingers. 'I think I broke my fist.'

The guard was out cold.

Jack turned with fear to the van, whose driver must have seen what had gone on in his mirror, and could still raise the alarm.

The van flashed its hazard-warning lights once, signalling to Jack. The driver could raise the alarm . . . but he wouldn't.

Jack gave him a wave and ran for the woods with Rapunzel.

They soon heard the sounds of alarm bells ringing.

'What do we do now?' asked Rapunzel.

Jack did not like to admit he hadn't thought that far ahead.

Just then, a beautiful woman in a sparkly blue dress appeared before them, carrying a carpet under her arm.

'Be not afraid,' said the woman. 'I'm yer Fairy Godmaw.'

'What are you doing here?' asked Jack.

'Isn't it obvious?' replied the Fairy Godmaw. 'I'm a plot device.' She fixed Jack with a steely glare. 'You had several more minutes of the time-freeze spell, but magic only works if you believe it, Son. Why did ye have to start doubting?'

'I think that was me,' shrugged Rapunzel.

The Fairy Godmaw sighed. 'I'm no supposed to dae this.' She rolled out the carpet on the forest floor, just as they heard a distant cry of "There they are!' and the sound of breaking twigs. 'Get on the carpet and tell it where ye want to go.'

'Thank you,' said Jack. He gathered Rapunzel onto the carpet and cried, 'Beanstalk!'

'Where?' asked Rapunzel.

But the carpet was already taking flight.

It wobbled in airborne waves beneath them, making Jack nauseous, although he tried not to show it.

'Jack,' said Rapunzel. 'Where are we going?'

Jack explained about the beanstalk as briefly as he could.

Rapunzel nodded, quite calmly. She had seen enough extraordinary things to make a beanstalk fairly easy to accept.

'But we must go to Upenda.'

'Punzy, Upenda's safest where she is,' Jack explained. 'They'll no deport her without you, but if you try and take her without permission, that's abduction, and you could both get deported. I know it's hard, but your best bet is to keep a low profile until yer lawyer gets back.'

'No, you don't understand,' said Rapunzel. 'You don't know – can't know – what danger she's in. He'll find her.'

'Who?'

'Look, Jack, I can't tell you everything. But . . . can't you phone her?'

'Dunno if the signal would interfere wi' the magic carpet,' said Jack.

Rapunzel shot him a glare.

'It was a joke!' Jack insisted, taking out his mobile. 'Tell you what I'll dae . . . I'll phone Ella on her mobile.' He did so. 'Hi, Ella, it's Jack. Is Upenda there? What's going on? You sound like you're scrubbing a dozen horrible dogs . . . Oh. That'll be why, then. Listen, is Upenda with you . . . ? Can you get her?' He looked up at Rapunzel. 'She'll just be a minute . . . Oh, hi, Upenda. Listen, don't ask questions. I have your mother with me, and she wants to talk to you.'

Rapunzel snatched the phone from Jack. 'Upenda? Upenda, darling, how are you? Are you alright? Are they treating you well? Has . . . *he* come to you? . . . That is good. You know what to do if he does? . . . Good. I love you.' Rapunzel listened to her daughter speak for a few minutes, tears spilling down her cheeks. 'Listen, I must go. You be brave, and remember that I love you, and that everything will be alright. Okay. Goodbye.'

She hung up.

When she had gathered herself together, she looked into Jack's eyes. 'Are you sure you know what you're doing with the beanstalk idea? I mean, how do you know it will not reject you as it rejected all others who have tried to get near? And what about me?'

'I cannae explain,' said Jack. 'You've just got to have faith. I know that I'm the only one who can climb it. It's my destiny. Everything will be alright if we go up there. I know it.'

'But even if you can climb the beanstalk, surely I cannot?'

'I think that as long as you're touching me, you can get inside the force field. Just keep holding my hand and you'll never fall.'

Rapunzel didn't look convinced.

Jack sighed. 'Look, I'm desperate to know what's up there, okay?'

'Now we're getting to the truth.'

'The polis have the area cordoned off. This is probably my only chance to get near the beanstalk.'

'So you are using me to satisfy your own curiosity.' She broke into a huge, cheek-inflating grin. 'I should be angry, you know.'

'Punzy, if you don't want to go, we won't go. Assuming I can figure oot how to steer this thing . . . But in all honesty, I can't think of anywhere else we can go.'

'I think it is a mistake,' said Rapunzel, 'and I have learned to distrust magic of any sort. But I will go with you, because I love you.'

'That's sweet . . . but very scary,' mused Jack.

They had no time to discuss the matter further. The magic carpet turned upside down and sent them plummeting through the air, then sped off.

Both screamed as they fell through the air. Jack grabbed in order of priority: Rapunzel's wrist; then the first other thing that came to hand.

The latter was the stalk of a giant leaf, jutting out sideways from the giant beanstalk.

When they had steadied themselves, Jack looked outwards. He could see the entire city. They had to be some distance off the ground.

He noticed a structure nearby that looked familiar, but he couldn't quite identify it. Then he realised that the reason he hadn't recognised it at first was that he had never seen the top of it before. It hadn't really occurred to him that there was such an angle.

The Finnieston Crane.

'Well,' he said, looking up and seeing that they were less than halfway to the distant top of the beanstalk. 'The only way is up!'

There were enough leaves sticking out, enough vines as thick as ropes dangling down, that climbing was a relatively simple matter at first . . . providing one didn't dwell too much on the size of the drop. The tricky part for the climbers was holding onto each other's hands while climbing, for if Rapunzel lost contact with Jack, she would fall.

It started to rain. Every time Jack tried to get purchase with his boots upon the smooth, wet surface of the beanstalk, he slipped and slid, and would have fallen if not for clinging on tightly to a vine.

The only way up after the rain began was for Jack to grab a handhold and pull himself up with one hand, then lift the entire weight of Rapunzel with the other, and swing his legs up without ever letting go of Rapunzel's hand.

The higher they got, the more violently the wind made the beanstalk lurch from side to side, as if the gods themselves were trying to shake the couple loose.

At one point Rapunzel lost her footing completely, and dangled from Jack's muscular grip.

'Hold on tight!' Jack yelled to her.

'Great idea!' she called back. 'I hadn't thought of that!'

Jack pulled her up to the relative safety of the branch he was on and kissed her. 'Come on. The sooner we get to the top, the sooner we can . . . erm . . . just come on!'

Jack heard a distant rumble of thunder and his heart beat so hard it hurt. It had not occurred to him until then, but if lightning hit the beanstalk, they were finished.

'Come on, let's go!' he roared.

'Excuse me,' said Rapunzel, 'do you actually think that's going to make me climb faster?'

Jack marvelled at her cheek, muttering to himself, 'I shoulda left her there.'

The beanstalk was tapering, and soon became narrow enough that between the two of them, they could get their arms right around it. So hugging it tightly between their arms and holding fast to each other's wrists, squeezing the beanstalk between their thighs, they inched their way up.

Finally, they reached a plateau of soft, cloud-like ground that stretched before them.

Jack patted the ground with his hand. 'It's okay,' he said, 'I think we can walk on it.'

They took their first tentative steps on the physically impossible, solid cloud that stretched as far as the eye could see.

'I don't know what I was expecting,' Jack grumbled. 'But this wasnae it.'

'This will do fine,' said Rapunzel, sitting down. 'I am glad of the chance to sit.'

Rapunzel unpacked her hair from her jumper and spun her head round several times until her hair was in its usual style, piled up high upon her head, but revealing little clue about its extraordinary length.

Seeing her do this made Jack think of how much he loved her hair, which made him think about how much he loved . . . everything about her, which made him blurt out, 'Marry me, Punzy!' before he could stop himself.

Her reaction was far from what he had hoped: she burst into tears.

'Hey, ssh!' said Jack. He stooped to put an arm around her. 'It's not that horrible an idea, is it?'

'I'm sorry,' bubbled Rapunzel. 'It's just . . . it's too much! Too much for one day!' She sobbed loudly and hugged herself. 'I've been a prisoner. I've been free. I've seen impossible things and climbed to the top of one of them. Now I am as tired as I've ever been, and you ask me to marry you.'

'I'm sorry,' said Jack. 'I'm sorry, I . . . I should have thought.'

'So tired,' said Rapunzel, 'and so cold.' She hugged herself even tighter, and shivered. Jack took half his jacket off, and put his free arm around her waist. Rapunzel put her arm into Jack's empty sleeve. 'Thank you,' she said.

They lay like that for a while, and Rapunzel said, 'Jack . . . you talk of marriage . . . but there is no guarantee I will be allowed to stay in Scotland.'

'Wherever you go, I'll go with you,' said Jack.

'In my country, the king himself wants me dead. If you go with me, you will die too.'

'Beats living without you.'

They were silent for a time, and eventually Jack realised that Rapunzel was sleeping. It didn't take him long to fall asleep too.

CHAPTER 8

Upenda awoke in the night, startled by a strange sound.

But, no. It was more than that. She could hear breathing and there was a definite shape . . . like a short, hooded figure. She stopped breathing herself for a second to listen. No doubt about it. She was not alone in the darkness.

She turned on the bedside lamp. That ordinarily chased the shadows away and reassured her that the shapes were nothing but everyday objects.

But there really was a short, hooded figure by her bed.

Its eyes glowed red from under its hood, and it reached out a greyish, skeletal hand towards her.

'You have been removed from your mother's protection,' it hissed. 'You are mine now.'

Upenda sat bolt-upright and stabbed a finger at the creature. '*I know your name!*' she cried.

The creature started, took a step back, its decaying hands held up defensively as if the child were shining a bright light into its eyes. 'That will keep you safe for now, but not for long. You must know that the power of that word is diminishing. Soon, without your mother, you will be beyond its help.'

There was a soft knock at the bedroom door and Ella's voice whispered, 'Upenda, are you alright?'

On hearing another's voice, the creature vanished in a puff of smoke.

'I'm fine,' said Upenda. 'I just had a bad dream.'

'Can I come in?'

'Sure.'

Ella came in, smiled kindly at the child, and sat at the edge of the bed.

'It's a horrible feeling when ye've just had a bad dream, isn't it?' asked Ella. 'And, like, ye cannae get back to sleep, but ye cannae get rid of the horrible atmosphere. The feeling, the smell, the fear.'

'Aye,' said Upenda. 'That's what it is like.'

Ella nodded. 'I've had plenty o' those. But it's no real, and it goes away after a while. Do ye want me to stay for a wee while?'

'Yes. Are you sure it's okay?'

'Of course. I don't mind.'

'Thank you.'

A few moments passed, then Ella said, in a hushed whisper, 'Knock knock?'

'Who's there?'

'Panda.'

'Panda who?'

'Panda Monium!'

Upenda giggled. 'That was bad.'

'If it was that bad, why are you laughing?'

Upenda shrugged. Then she said, 'Knock knock?'

'Who's there?'

'Boo.'

'Boo who?'

'Don't cry, it's only a joke!'

Ella chuckled. 'And you said mine was bad? I've got one. Knock-knock?'

'Who's there?'

'Interrupting cow.'

'Interrupting c—'

'MOOOOOOOOO!'

Upenda giggled away, temporarily forgetting about her encounter with her family's oldest enemy.

They shared knock-knock jokes until Upenda's failure to giggle signalled that she had fallen asleep.

Then Ella crept back to her own room, leaving the light on.

'Jack! Jack, wake up!'

Jack awoke from a strange dream to an even stranger reality, which had grown stranger still while he was sleeping.

A castle stood before his bleary eyes where none had been when he fell asleep.

'Wow,' said Jack, wondering how to respond to this surreal vision. Eventually he settled on, 'Erra castle, by the way.'

'So I see,' said Rapunzel. 'How do you feel?'

'Ready to face my destiny,' Jack insisted in a breathless whisper. 'How about you?'

'Sick of the sight of castles.' She swallowed hard, then looked at Jack, attempting a confident smile. 'Shall we . . .?'

He took her hand and they approached the door to the castle. The closer they came, the clearer it became that the entrance was very, very large . . . and slightly ajar.

'Jack, I don't like this,' said Rapunzel. 'What sort of person needs such a large door?'

'A very large person,' said Jack, 'but we cannae turn back noo.'

'It is not right to enter someone's home uninvited.'

'But this isnae someone else's home,' insisted Jack. 'I planted this beanstalk. My beanstalk. My castle. And above all, my destiny.'

'You keep saying that word as if it means something,' said Rapunzel. 'Destiny is just stuff that is going to happen.'

Jack crossed his arms sulkily. 'If I thought something meant a lot to you, I'd do anything to help.'

Rapunzel rolled her eyes.

'I'll tell you what,' said Jack. 'I'll knock on the door. If there's nae answer, we'll go in. If someone tells us to sod off, we sod off. Fair?'

'And if a giant comes out and throws us both off the beanstalk?'

Jack grinned. 'Then I promise I'll never say the word "destiny" to you ever again.'

'That isn't funny,' said Rapunzel. She looked at her feet in an effort to hide her smile.

'Then why are you laughing?'

'I'm not laughing,' said Rapunzel, unable to talk and fight the spreading grin at the same time. 'Okay, I may be smiling a bit, but I am certainly not laughing.'

'You're as curious as I am, aren't you?'

'I'm . . . a *little* bit curious,' replied Rapunzel, cautiously.

Jack took a deep breath, knocked on the door and waited.

'Nae answer,' he said.

Rapunzel poked her head in the door. 'Hello?' she called. 'Is anyone home?' Her voice echoed back. 'We have travelled a long way and need shelter. Can we come in?'

A voice other than Rapunzel's echo called back from within the castle. It cried 'HELP!'

'Sounds like an invitation to me,' said Jack.

'Aye,' Rapunzel agreed and they dashed in as one.

Along stone-built corridors they dashed, surrounded by the deafening thunder of their own echoing footsteps. The walls were lined with suits of armour and paintings of scary people, and the air smelled of blood, sweat and very old books.

'HELP!' cried the voice, and they followed it to a great chamber with a four-poster bed in the centre that was much bigger than a double-decker bus. Crystal lanterns and silver-framed mirrors adorned the walls, and a huge chandelier dangled magnificently from the ceiling.

A rock in a corner, with a sword sticking out of it, looked out of place.

By the bed was a man-sized cage with an ostrich in it, and, on top of that, a tiny, tiny cage with a tiny young woman in it, no bigger than Jack's thumb.

'Don't just stand there. Get us out of here!' hissed the tiny woman.

'Right,' said Jack.

'Poor thing,' cooed Rapunzel, stroking the beak of the ostrich through the bars of its cage. A poor thing it was indeed, for the cage was far too small for it. Its wings were pressed against its sides, its neck was bent to squeeze it in, and it was sitting on a growing pile of golden eggs.

'BWAARKH!' said the ostrich in a friendly way.

'You are adorable,' said Rapunzel. 'Can we keep her?'

'Gonnae just get us out of here?' hissed the tiny one. 'The giant will be back any minute.'

'Awright, keep yer hair on,' said Jack, trying to pull the door off the tiny cage. It was stronger than it looked.

'Use the sword, you moron!' spat the tiny woman.

'What is it wi' women I rescue? They've all got an attitude problem!'

Nonetheless, he crossed the room to the sword in the stone and read the inscription aloud: 'Only the true King of the Beanstalk can remove this sword.'

'Aye,' said the tiny woman. 'The giant's been trying for years to nab it, but he's had nae luck. Must no be the true king.'

The ground shook. The chandelier rattled. Huge footsteps thundered down the corridor.

The ostrich was so afraid, it laid another golden egg.

'Hide!' whispered Jack, grabbing Rapunzel by the hand and dragging her under the bed.

'You're supposed to grab the sword first, Brainiac!' cried the tiny woman in despair.

The door of the giant's bedroom flew open.

From Jack's hiding place, he caught a glimpse of the hideous beast: an incredibly ugly giant of a man with a chewed-up nose, beady eyes and hair like a jungle. And as for his size . . . Jack and Rapunzel could both fit comfortably into one of his boots (if they could only stand the smell).

'FEE FIE FO FUM!' cried the giant. 'I SMELL THE BLOOD OF AN ENGLISHMAN!'

'I'm no English!' cried an outraged Jack, realising an instant too late that he had given himself away.

'Too thick to live,' the tiny woman concluded gloomily, shaking her head.

'WORKS EVERY TIME,' boomed the giant, and he plucked Jack from under the bed and popped him in his giant mouth.

It all went very dark.

Very dark, very wet and very smelly.

Only by clinging fast to a gigantic mouth ulcer did Jack escape being swallowed.

Jack fumbled for Jill's phone, which had a built-in torch, turned it on and flooded the giant's oral cavity with light, while wrestling desperately with the giant's huge, slimy tongue. He kicked against the teeth, rapidly losing hope of survival.

Then he saw hope; one of the giant's teeth had a giant filling.

In the instant before he was crunched like a pretzel, Jack produced a set of metal keys and jammed them hard against the filling.

The giant roared with the distinctive pain of 'filling shock', and Jack saw a parting of his lips just big enough to jump through.

As luck would have it, Jack landed on the soft bed, and so escaped serious injury. He untucked the giant sheet, slid down it to the floor, then made a run for the sword.

The giant moved to chase his much smaller enemy, but in his haste failed to notice that Rapunzel had wrapped her hair around his legs.

Jack pulled the sword out easily and held it up, just as the giant fell face-first upon it. In an instant, he was dead.

Jack wiped his sword on the dead giant's clothes while Rapunzel retrieved her hair.

'I thought you were dead,' cried Rapunzel, flinging her arms around him. Jack barely seemed to notice.

The King of the Beanstalk wasted no time in using his sword to open the cages of the tiny woman and the ostrich. The ostrich nuzzled him gratefully.

Jack's world was spinning; giant or no, he had just killed someone. That was a lot to take in. Everything that had happened since he went to Dungavel was a lot to take in. He suddenly realised that Rapunzel was holding him up.

'Are you okay?'

'None of us will be okay if we don't get oot o' here,' cried the tiny woman.

The ground trembled and the mirrors and chandelier began to shatter. Lightning seemed to streak across the ceiling. 'See that giant? See his existential life-energy that comes fae the Magical Realm? It was mystically linked to the cohesive life force o' the entire beanstalk!'

'What?' cried an increasingly befuddled Jack, as the alarmed ostrich laid yet another golden egg.

'Let's see if I can put it in words even you'd unnerstaun,' snapped the tiny woman. 'Um . . . see this beanstalk? It's aboot to explode!'

'What?' cried Rapunzel, her eyes wide. 'We have to get out of here, now!'

'Wish I'd thought o' that!' said the tiny woman.

Jack gathered his wits about him. This was, indeed a serious predicament.

He picked up the tiny woman and stuck her in his shirt pocket.

'I'm Thumbelina, by the way,' said the tiny woman. 'Everyone cries me Thumbsy.'

'I'm Jack,' said Jack. 'This is Rapunzel. Pleased to meet ye. We're riding out of here on the ostrich.' With that, he boarded the bird.

'I'm destined to marry the King of the Pixies,' said Thumbsy, almost conversationally. 'Ostriches cannae fly, by the way.'

'I know,' said Jack, as Rapunzel climbed up behind him and put her arms around his middle, 'but they can run awfae fast.'

'Doon a beanstalk?!'

'Let's find out! YAH! YAH!'

The ostrich laid another golden egg and charged forth, dashing along the castle's corridors which were collapsing around them.

Clearing the castle, Jack and Rapunzel dared not look behind them as they heard the roar of the explosion.

The ostrich seemed to know what to do: it dived down the hole in the floor of solid cloud, and charged at incredible speed, in a spiral pattern, round and down the beanstalk, its feet momentarily touching a branch or vine with every brief step.

The wind threatened to wrench Jack from the back of the ostrich. The round-and-round motion of its run made him dizzy and nauseous. He heard what he thought was wind . . . no, it wasn't wind. He felt the heat and saw the light reflected on the ground below. The beanstalk was exploding, a foot at a time, right above his head. They were only one step ahead of the blast.

'The answer is yes,' Rapunzel yelled over the wind.

'What?' cried Jack, who was distracted by their probable imminent death.

'Yes, I will marry you!'

Jack instantly forgot their probable imminent death, and his nausea, and let a roar of triumph fill the exploding Glasgow sky.

'Big deal,' grumbled Thumbsy from his shirt pocket. 'I'm destined to marry the King of the Pixies.'

They landed on what was left of the Squinty Bridge just before the explosion hit the Clyde and sent gallons of water and tons of bridge flying in every direction.

They crashed through the police cordon, much to the astonishment of the policeman on duty, who quickly adjusted his hat and said, 'Excuse me, Sir, is this your ostrich?'

Jack dropped the sword and dismounted, as did Rapunzel, as the sound of blaring sirens drew nearer.

'This is low profile, right?' asked Rapunzel.

* * *

'SCANDAL! ASYLUM CHEAT ESCAPES AND GETS LEAVE TO REMAIN', cried one hysterical headline.

'ASYLUM CROOK CAMERON GETS MULTI-MILLION MOVIE DEAL', complained another.

'WHAT HAPPENED UP THERE, ANYWAY?' wondered a third.

One newspaper even decided to sculpt reality a little: 'ASYLUM FRAUD IN BRIDGE BANG INVESTIGATION: POLICE UNABLE TO PROVE TERROR LINK.'

But for the most part, Glasgow took the whole thing in its stride:

'I see that beanstalk's away.'

'Oh, aye. Blew up, so it did.'

'What d'ye reckon happened to it?'

'Och, just wan o' they things, i'nt it?'

'Aye. Some weather we've been getting, eh?'

As for Jack, Rapunzel, Upenda and Thumbsy, things went rather well for them after that.

Jack was questioned at length by police about the sword and the beanstalk, but they had to accept his story, for there was no evidence to disprove it.

He did get a movie deal for his extraordinary story, and between that and his ostrich that laid the golden eggs, he was a rich man.

Rapunzel was released, and reunited with Upenda.

Jack and Rapunzel bought a doll's house for Thumbsy, who reminded them that she was destined to marry the King of the Pixies as often as possible.

Life was good, but to say that they lived happily ever after would, at this stage, be premature.

CHAPTER 9

Wee Red Hoodie made the mistake of muttering under her breath in front of her granny.

'You dare swear at me?'

'I wasnae swearing,' Red pleaded. 'Honest I wasnae.'

'And noo you're lying to me?'

'No!' Red started to cry. She hated herself for it. Anything was better than crying in front of Granny.

Spurred on by this sign of weakness, Granny grabbed Red by the hair.

'We all know what happens to wee lassies that swear and tell lies, don't we?'

The old woman dragged her granddaughter to the bathroom and washed her mouth out with soap, then gave her a couple of kicks for good measure.

Red crawled back through to the living room.

'Ye'll get my shopping for me,' Granny informed her and wrote out an illegible list, which she handed to Red.

Red despaired. 'So what have I to get?'

'Can ye no read?'

Red took a deep breath and prepared for the inevitable. 'It's a wee bit hard to read your writing.'

Granny shoved the pencil, rubber-end-first, right up Red's nose.

'Go!' the old woman screamed. 'And don't you dare forget anything!'

* * *

Red sniffed and snorted and snorted and sniffed. The discomfort of having had something rammed up her nose lingered.

She clenched her fists and bit her lips, determined not to cry, but her eyes filled with water.

She leaned against a lamppost saying, 'I wish she would die! I wish the horrible old bag would just die!'

'That's a rather indiscreet thing to say, if you don't mind my saying so,' came a voice.

Startled, she looked around her.

'Who's there?' she asked, shaking with fear.

'I apologise for not showing myself,' said the voice. 'I fear my appearance would frighten you.'

'Leave me alone,' insisted the youngster, and crossed to the other side of the road.

In the next moment a wolf was in front of her; a wolf whose face was burned in places and who was missing patches of fur. Red screamed.

The Wolf's paw was over her mouth in an instant.

'I did warn you,' said the Wolf. 'Now, calm down, stop struggling and I'll release you.'

She did and he did.

'Good,' the wolf went on. 'Now, tell me more about this wish of yours, to see an "old bag" dead?'

'That's nane o' your business!' spat the child, fearful now that she might be told on.

'Of course not,' the Wolf remarked, casually. 'Just seems a strange thing to say in this city in the current climate. Most people have grown extremely wary of wishing out loud, since the mysterious beanstalk saga became the biggest news story. Especially wishes one might . . . rather not come true.'

'Aye, well . . .' Red crossed her arms. 'Who says I'd rather it didnae?'

'My dear child, let us be candid with each other. Do you or don't you want your grandmother to die?'

[87]

'Aye. Well, naw. Well, sometimes. Look, you don't know what it's like for me.'

'Oh, but I do,' said the Wolf. 'I've been watching you. I know how you've suffered at the hands of that monster. I would not blame you at all if you were moved to . . . desperate measures.'

Red shrugged. 'So?'

'So . . . what if I said I could help you? What if I said that I could make your granny disappear forever? All you have to do is nod?'

'I'd say ye were a psycho. Now, I'm in a hurry.'

'Ahh, but if you give me the nod,' said the Wolf, 'you would not have to hurry. The beating you'd get – whether late or not – would never happen. Trust me.'

Something in his voice did make her trust him. It was a gentle, reassuring, velvety voice; the sort of voice that can tell you everything's going to be alright, and you believe it.

'Think about it,' said the Wolf, circling her now. 'You are close to the beginning of your life. She is near the end of hers. She hates your freedom, and I can feel your yearning, your aching to be free.'

She frowned and tried to radiate indifference with her body language. 'So what?'

'So, she has caused you nothing but pain. Surely you don't feel compassion towards her? Surely you don't . . . *love* her?'

'What ye asking me to dae?'

'Nothing you don't want to,' replied the Wolf, mimicking her nonchalance. 'If you want to reclaim your life, to be free of that wicked woman forever . . . just nod. I only ask you to agree that at some point in the future, you will do me a favour. What do you say?'

Red didn't know what to say. It was tempting; a life without Granny. She had never met a talking wolf before. Much less a talking wolf willing to do a murder for her.

There was a constant pain deep inside her nose. She snorted and sniffed and sniffed and snorted and snorted and sniffed and . . . spat.

Out came the rubber from the top of that pencil, covered in bogeys and blood, that had been trapped in her sinuses all this time.

She gave the Wolf a look of daggers and ice. She nodded.

'Excellent choice,' said the Wolf. 'I suggest you go and enjoy some junk food at your grandmother's expense, whilst I make certain she won't mind.'

Red sat with her cheeseburger and cola. She had never felt so alone.

She had managed to convince a part of her mind that what was going on wasn't real: that the Big, Bad Wolf was not swallowing her gran.

Because if he was . . . she was guilty of murder.

So this is what it feels like to be a murderer, she thought to herself. It didn't feel much different from being a non-murderer. That was strange.

But she wasn't a murderer. Not really. At least, she might not be. It depended, she supposed, on whether the Wolf was serious. Or whether he was real, come to that. Maybe she had imagined him. Maybe she was dreaming.

If she was a murderer . . . shouldn't that bother her? It didn't. Yet it bothered her that it didn't bother her. Certainly she felt no pity for her gran. Why should she?

Red sighed. It wasn't surprising to her that she was capable of murder. She knew she was bad. Granny had told her often enough. Just born bad.

She put it out of her mind, and decided it was too far-fetched that the Big, Bad Wolf was really eating her granny on her orders. She would go home, get beaten up for stealing the shopping money to buy junk food, and life would be back to normal. Soon she would forget all about the Big, Bad Wolf.

The Wolf made short work of Granny, taking out his own frustrations upon her. He felt quite satisfied.

Now, the Wolf had a peculiar sense of humour, which took over his reason now and again, and this was one of those times. He tried to imagine how Red would respond to finding him, in her gran's rocking chair, wearing her gran's clothes, under a blanket. She would either see the funny side or the horrific side: either way it would give the Wolf a giggle.

He heard the key turning in the door and felt a thrill of excitement.

The front door creaked open.

'Granny?' the child called from the hallway. 'Granny, are you there?'

'Come in, my dear,' said the Wolf, in a ghastly parody of the old woman's voice.

'Granny?' There was a note of uncertainty in Red's voice. 'Granny, is that you?'

'Come through to the living room,' said the Wolf. 'I want to hit you with my walking stick and make you drink sour milk.'

Red crept cautiously into the living room. She half-knew it was not her granny's voice she had heard.

When she saw the Wolf wearing Granny's clothes, she felt an extraordinary sense of relief. Strangely, knowing the old woman was dead stopped her worrying about it, and she knew she was not going to get a beating this time.

She laughed and laughed, loving the incongruity of the hairy, half-cooked wolf in her granny's clothes.

'Oh, Granny!' she cried, caught up in the hilarity and excitement. 'What big eyes ye've got!'

'All the better to see you with, my dear,' said the Wolf, still mocking Granny's voice.

'And Granny,' Red managed between breathless giggles, 'what big ears ye've got!'

To which the Wolf replied, 'Pardon?'

Red was in such hysterics that she only just managed to squeeze out the words, 'What big teeth you have!'

The Wolf then leapt out of the reclining chair, crying, 'All the better to EAT THE OLD BAG!'

They exchanged a high-five and roared with laughter.

'So how are you feeling?' said the Wolf. 'No problems with your conscience, I take it?'

'My what?'

'No feelings of guilt?'

'Nah,' said Red, with a cruel shrug. 'Like ye says, she had it coming.'

'That's the spirit,' said the Wolf. 'Then that concludes our business for now. I will be in touch at some point to collect the favour you owe me, but in the meantime . . . your life is yours.'

The trouble was that Red soon found she didn't much care for her life being hers. She had longed for it, dreamed of it, but freedom isn't worth much without something to do with it, and she had nothing.

She found she couldn't stomach living in the flat where Gran had died. Besides, someone would find her there eventually, take her into care, or worse.

So she started squatting in abandoned buildings, making friends with others who had found their freedom, throwing things at buses, drinking Buckfast and smashing bottles just to stave off the boredom.

No one loved her. No one respected her. Those who noticed her despised her.

Gran had never loved or respected her, and probably did despise her, but she at least had given her some attention.

Then there were the nightmares.

Every night, she would see her own hands around her granny's throat, squeezing the life out of her, wanting to stop but unable to.

She would wake up screaming 'It wasnae me! I didnae do anything! All I did was nod!'

She refused to feel guilty when she was awake. All she did was nod . . . besides, the old bag had it coming. She had tortured Red, humiliated her, taken away her chance in life.

But guilt still existed in Red and it caught up with her in dreams. So she did her best not to sleep.

It wasn't much of a life.

So when the Wolf caught up with her she was dazed and bedraggled, wandering the streets of Glasgow, pestering people for change.

'So this is what you are doing with freedom?' he asked.

'Go away,' she replied.

'Well, that's gratitude for you,' said the Wolf. 'Tell you what . . . why don't I take you somewhere better?'

She shrugged and followed him.

She wasn't sure where the Wolf was leading her, but she wasn't expecting it to be down a manhole.

Nevertheless, she lowered herself down and followed the Wolf through a labyrinth of tunnels and holes in the floor.

'Where are we going?' she asked. She was becoming frightened. This was a wolf with no qualms about killing. What if she was about to share her grandmother's fate? She shrugged when she realised she probably deserved as much, and struggled to pull herself through some of the tight passages.

'Try to keep up, my dear,' said the Wolf, who was navigating with ease.

When she came to a large clearing, she had to blink a few times before she could take in what she saw.

'This is where I live,' the Wolf remarked casually. 'It's not much, but it's home.'

Red looked around her, awestruck. The room was circular and lit with several lamps. It was also huge; possibly the biggest room she had ever been in.

In the middle was a fountain, splashing into a swimming pool. Furnishings included a cinema-sized television, a three-piece suite, several fridges and a very large beanbag.

'This is amazing,' said Red. 'How . . . ?'

'Oh, it's easy when you've got money and time. You see, my dear, as I have constructed my empire, one dirty job at a time . . . built my reputation as a force to be reckoned with, never messed with, and an uncanny talent for getting things done discreetly . . . I've managed to build my home from a single section of a disused sewer . . . to this, a bit at a time.'

She looked around her, eyes wide, touching this, stroking that.

The Wolf laughed softly. 'You're free to stay here as long as you please. To come and go as you please. To raid the fridges, watch the television, surf the Net . . . and if you have any other needs or desires, you have only to ask. I will treat you as I would my own cub.'

A moment ago, Red had been just another anonymous ned; a nobody. Now, she lived in an underground palace, and more importantly . . . she meant something to someone. She was going to be looked after.

Yet she had the queasiest feeling in her stomach. This was the creature who had killed her granny, after all. On her orders, true, but still . . . the Wolf was responsible for those horrible nightmares, as much as she herself was. She had almost convinced herself that she hadn't done what she did, hadn't really given him any signal, hadn't really believed he would actually do it . . . it was entirely the Wolf's doing and none of hers. Yet she was grateful to him. She felt no guilt over the death of her gran: why should she? She was born bad.

And what of the favour she had promised, without really knowing what would be asked of her?

'Mr Wolf,' she said, slightly hesitantly. 'You said I'd have to dae ye a favour . . .'

'Oh, come, now,' said the Wolf. 'Let's not think about that just yet. Let's think about your new life! No school, no bedtime, no adults telling you what you can and can't eat, what you can and can't watch on telly. You must be starving. Would you like a slice of chocolate cake?' He opened one of the fridges to reveal an endless landscape of sumptuous desserts, with a huge chocolate gateau as its centrepiece.

'Perhaps,' continued the Wolf as the child gaped. 'You'd care for an entire chocolate cake? Or . . . several chocolate cakes?'

'I'm gonnae like this new life,' she breathed. 'But . . . I think I'll take the chocolate cakes wan at a time.'

CHAPTER 10

'It's today,' Ella breathed when the sunlight woke her up.

The day had, indeed, arrived. The day of the ball.

Nothing Kara, Clara or their father said sunk in. The ball was all she could think about.

She, Ella McCinder, had a ticket to Harry Charmaine's charity ball. She, wee Ella McCinder . . . was actually going to meet Harry Charming!

She was still worried about her clothes. Her Fairy Godmaw had assured her it would be fine, but . . . what if the magic didn't work? What if there was something else she had to do? What if she had completely misunderstood?

The only clothes she had remotely clean were what she was wearing: her torn jeans, her last-season's Celtic top, and her Velcro-fastening, tatty, pink trainers. Not exactly dressed to kill.

Since she had stepped between her foster family and Upenda, they had indeed treated the child well . . . but had been particularly cruel to Ella. It was as if she had declared all-out war. She knew her clothes would get mankier as the day went on, for they would make her do the most disgusting jobs they could think of.

Sometimes she felt so nervous she was almost sick. Other times she was so elated she could barely keep from bouncing, and she whistled while she scrubbed the gutters with a toothbrush.

She was going to meet Harry Charmaine! What possible punishment could take the shine off that?

In the cellar, which hadn't been cleaned in years, she was sorting junk into boxes and scrubbing the walls and floor. There was a musty smell she barely noticed.

A spider scuttled across the floor.

'I'll get ye oot o' here soon, wee spider,' Ella told it, kindly. 'Soon as the coast is clear. If that lot saw ye, they'd step on ye soon as look at ye.'

Suddenly, the cellar door creaked open, and her foster father cast his huge shadow across the floor.

'I'm driving my daughters to the ball,' he said. 'I shan't be long. I expect you to keep working down here.'

'Yes, Sir,' said Ella, thinking, *Is it that time already?*

'Ugh,' he said, 'the smell in here is absolutely appalling.'

That gave Ella a brainwave. She turned away so he couldn't see her grinning from ear to ear as she realised that he wouldn't return to the cellar at all that evening.

'It's going to take me all night to do this, you know,' she told him.

'So be it,' he replied, slamming the door. Ella heard the giggling of Kara and Clara above, then heard the front door close and the family car start up and drive off.

Ella stood in silence, waiting for . . . what was she waiting for?

'Now what?' she asked no one in particular. So much of her plan was finely balanced on a tightrope of faith.

'Now,' said the spider, expanding to her height and turning into a chauffeur, 'You stick a courgette out front like you said you would. And don't dilly dally, we haven't got all day.'

Ella hugged him and rushed upstairs, taking care to close the cellar door behind her.

She rummaged in the vegetable rack for a courgette, and put it out in the driveway. Instantly it transformed into a big, pink limo.

'That's impressive,' said Ella.

'Not really,' said the chauffeur. 'If a spider drove you to the ball in a courgette . . . now that would be impressive.'

'You've got a point,' giggled Ella. 'Oh, God, what aboot my claithes?'

'Oh, ye of little faith!' said the chauffeur.

Ella felt her clothes moving, their fabrics wriggling and writhing against her skin. She felt her shoes change shape around her feet, and become quite uncomfortable. She almost fell over as they quite suddenly grew high heels. When she looked down, she was wearing the most beautiful, jewel-encrusted, golden shoes she had ever seen in her life.

Her clothes weren't done changing shape. Her jeans and her Celtic top had merged, and were changing texture and colour. Soon she was wearing a grand, flowing dress that made its magnificent way up her body in spirals, layer after layer, pink upon gold upon pink.

The watch on her wrist, which was now ruining the look of the outfit, shimmered and vanished.

Her hair lost its straggly, greasy inelegance, piling itself up high in lovely golden curls.

The dress was far enough off her shoulders that she could prise open a space at her collarbone and have a sniff at an armpit. She did not offend herself in the least! The spell, it seemed, included a personal dry-clean.

'Oh, this is good,' she told the chauffeur.

'Only the best for you, Madam,' he replied, opening the back door of the limo.

She got in, and found she had more room all to herself than she knew what to do with. There was a full-sized mirror straight ahead of her. Staring back at her was a beautiful woman, with poise and elegance, who was dressed just perfectly to go to the ball.

'Don't forget,' said the chauffeur when he dropped her off. 'You must leave the ball by midnight.'

For the entirety of the delicious five-course meal, Ella found herself sitting next to Kara, who had Clara on her other side.

They're going to recognise me, she told herself, heart pounding, but her head stayed high, for once.

'Excuse me,' said Kara. 'I hope you don't think I'm being rude . . . I was admiring your dress. Where did you get it?'

Ella was confused a moment. Kara was talking to her nicely . . . admiringly. She had identified Ella as somebody worth knowing. *She has no idea who I am*, she squealed inwardly.

'This?' said Ella. 'Nothing special, I just threw it on. You should see the rest of my wardrobe.'

Kara chuckled reluctantly.

'I like your dress,' said Ella.

'Oh, thank you,' Kara replied.

'Very nice. Ye make it yersel'?'

Clara sniggered at that, before an elbow from her sister made her think better of it.

Still Ella's heart wouldn't slow down. Apart from Reggie King, she had never met a celebrity before. Now she was surrounded by them! And there, only a few seats down was Reggie King, who was staring at her in a way she didn't like. Was her Fairy Godmaw wrong? Did he recognise her after all?

Where was Harry?

Soon the meal was over and the dancing began in earnest.

Harry seemed to be . . . hiding in a corner, talking to the Scotland manager. He didn't seem to want to mingle with his fans. For a moment, she thought she saw him looking at her, but when she looked up, he looked away.

He was hissing to his manager, 'Go find out who she is. Please.'

The manager hissed back, 'If you want to talk to her, go and talk to her.'

'I cannae!'

'How no?'

'I just cannae!'

'You're unbelievable! You'll happily slide-tackle Wayne Rooney, but you're feart to go up and talk to a lassie?'

'Too late noo, anyway,' said Charmaine, a note of relief in his voice. 'Look. There's Reggie King asking her to dance.'

Ella felt a touch at her elbow and spun to find herself facing Reggie King.

'I'm sorry,' King said, flashing her a charming smile. 'I didnae mean to startle you. I just . . . I could see ye were here by yersel', and I thought, "What's a beautiful lassie like that doing here all by hersel?" So I thought I'd come over and say hello.'

'Um, hello,' said Ella, giggling girlishly. Her mind was racing. She realised that King had no idea who she was and decided the safest thing to do would be to excuse herself and get away from him. She also thought she would never get a better opportunity to wind him up.

'Mr . . . ?' she asked, extending her hand.

King seemed taken aback. 'King,' he said, frowning, and forgetting to shake hands. 'You know, Reggie King, from *The Reggie King Show*. You must know who I am.'

'Oh,' said Ella. 'Are you on the telly, then?'

King realised that he was just standing with his mouth open, so he began to dance with her. 'Even if you don't watch my show, you must read newspapers.'

'Aye,' said Ella, dancing half-heartedly, 'but I tend to skim over the boring bits.'

'*Lipgloss* magazine voted me sexiest man in Britain three years running,' added King, determined to prove to this young lady that she had, indeed, heard of him.

'Och, I don't read *Lipgloss*,' said Ella (who had a subscription to the magazine, and had voted for Harry). 'It's just for silly wee lassies fawning over plain-faced celebrities.'

'Nae offence taken,' growled King.

'Och, I didnae mean *you*,' Ella told him playfully, daring to press his nose. 'You're a perfectly awright-looking bloke, I suppose. You're just no my type.'

'What do you mean, "not your type"?'

'Nae offence or that. I think you're awright. I just don't fancy ye.'

King tripped over his own feet, thrown off balance by this entirely new concept. He forced a laugh. 'Well, I think you'll find you're in a minority there, darling.'

'Aye, probably,' said Ella. 'So never mind, eh? Ye can still have almost any woman ye want.'

King tried to disguise his annoyance, but he twirled her a bit more fiercely than he was intending to and she almost lost her balance.

'Seriously, though,' said Ella, 'See the lassies that vote for the *Lipgloss* poll? I wouldnae take it as that much of a compliment, know what I'm saying? Most of them are too young for ye.'

They danced stiffly in silence for a time.

'Hey,' Ella cried suddenly. 'You must know Harry Charmaine!'

'Aye,' said King. 'I was interviewing him just the other week. On my show that everyone else watches.'

'Of course!' cried Ella, letting go of her dance partner long enough to snap her fingers. 'Sorry, I recognise ye now. You're that bloke who was interviewing Harry Charmaine on the telly! I'll watch anything he's on, you know? Sorry, what did ye say yer name was again?'

'King. Reginald King.'

'Sorry, Archibald,' said Ella. 'Don't suppose there's any chance you could . . . introduce me to Harry? I'm such a big fan of his.'

King had no chance to respond. He was flanked by Kara and Clara.

'Reggie King?' said Kara. 'I do hope we're not interrupting, but we are huge fans of yours and it is such an honour to meet you.'

'Yes, such an honour,' Clara echoed.

'Well, you really must excuse me,' King said to Ella, as much shoving her away as letting her go. 'I have fans to attend to.'

Ella turned away, a great big grin on her face, thinking, *I've ruined his whole night for him!*

She heard a nearby voice hiss, 'Look, just go and talk to her!'

When she turned she saw Harry Charmaine being physically pushed towards her.

'Um, hi,' Harry said.

'Hi,' said Ella.

Harry was staring at his shoes. 'I'm Harry Charmaine.'

Ella giggled and blushed. 'Aye. I know that.'

'I um . . . seen ye dancing wi' Reggie. You here wi' him?'

'Nah,' said Ella. 'I'm here mysel'.'

Harry smiled, but said nothing. He shifted awkwardly, wanting to talk to her, but no words came to him.

Am I no the wan that's supposed to get tongue-tied? she wondered. Aloud she said, 'Do ye want to dance wi' me?'

Harry grinned, blushed and shook his head. 'I cannae dance.'

'Och, don't talk daft!' laughed Ella. 'I see you dance every other week at Parkheid. Mair graceful than anyone on this flair!'

'Aye, that's different, but,' Harry shrugged awkwardly. 'If I've got a ball at my feet or that.'

Even this exchange was being widely noticed and photographed. Ella wondered for a moment if people who didn't recognise her in person would recognise her in a photo.

'Kid on ye've got a ball then,' she insisted, shrugging off the thought.

'I'm nae good at kidding on,' Harry insisted. 'I've nae imagination.'

'Och, see you!' cried Ella, thwacking his chest playfully. She pulled a balloon off the wall. 'Here . . . this is the ball.' She placed it under the toe of her golden shoe and worked it playfully this way and that. 'Now, tackle me, but dae it in time to the music.'

He took her hands and tried to snatch the balloon with his foot.

She heeled it up behind her, twirled and nosed it towards him. Then, as he moved to take the balloon on his thigh, she got in his way and controlled it with her chest, backing into him.

'You're the best footballer in Scotland,' giggled Ella, 'and you cannae get the ball aff a girl in high heels.'

'It's no a real ball, though,' said Harry.

They danced around each other in graceful pirouettes, taking the balloon from each other, dribbling, tackling, headering the balloon; keeping it close so they didn't move far from the spot. The balloon floated high into the air and slowly down again. It was like football in slow motion. It was dancing. It was beautiful.

No one else was dancing. All eyes and camera-flashes were upon the couple. Harry Charming and his mystery woman would dominate the next day's headlines, but they were oblivious.

Harry moved round behind her and put his arms around her waist, pinning her arms to her side. He got a knee through her legs and pushed her dress up to meet the falling balloon, knocking it into his hands.

'Now, that's definitely a foul,' she said.

She worked herself free, took the balloon from him, and playfully hit him on the forehead with it. Then she dropped it, rolled it under her foot, caught it on her heel . . .

BANG!

All the onlookers jumped and gasped. Then there was a roar of laughter, a thunder of applause and a flurry of flashes, and only then did the couple realise how much attention was focused on them.

'Oops,' Ella said, blushing furiously and wishing for a moment that her hair were loose so she could chew it a little . . . a habit she realised she ought to break.

'See, that's why we don't play football in high heels,' said Harry.

'What, no even in training?'

He laughed. 'So what are we gonnae dae for a ball noo?'

'Well if all else fails,' said Ella, taking his hands and closing the gap between them, 'we could aye just dance.'

'I tellt ye,' said Harry, 'I cannae dance.'

'And I proved ye wrang,' said Ella. 'Come on, it's easy. Just put yer arms aboot me and walk slowly in circles.'

He grinned. 'That I can do.' He slid his arms around her waist and she put hers around his neck.

She couldn't stop grinning. She was dancing with Harry Charmaine.

He liked her as much as she liked him, and he was just an ordinary, nice guy; an ordinary, nice guy who happened to have an extraordinary talent. That was so much more satisfying to her than the god of her dreams.

They followed the many eyes of the mirrorball in a slow circle. 'This is nice,' he said.

'Aye,' said Ella. 'It'll no win on *Strictly Come Dancing*, but it feels really nice.'

'You're amazing,' he whispered in her ear.

'Thanks.'

'I'd quite like to see you again sometime.'

'Aye,' she replied, trying not to tremble.

But before she could say more, she felt a strange tickling sensation on her wrist. She looked past Harry's neck and almost gasped in horror.

She broke away from Harry.

'What is it?' he asked.

Gazing at her wrist, she suddenly knew too well what it was. Her watch was reappearing. Her watch was reappearing because it was almost midnight. Soon her whole outfit would be changing back to the way it was.

'I've got to go,' she breathed in a panicked tone.

'Why? What's the matter?'

'I . . . I cannae explain. I just got to go.'

She backed away from him a bit, then turned and ran.

She dived into the toilet in such a hurry that she didn't realise it was the wrong toilet until she saw Reggie King at the urinal.

'Hello again,' said King, giving her a sidelong, puzzled glance.

'Sorry, Archibald, cannae stop and talk the noo,' she said breathlessly as she climbed on top of a wash-hand basin and hoisted herself through the window above. She gave a cry as her shoe got stuck in the window frame, and she fell down on the outside, the shoe on the inside.

Harry burst in just in time to see the last of her disappear and the shoe clatter into the wash-hand basin.

[102]

He climbed up and put his face to the window, ready to call after her
. . . but she hadn't told him her name.

'I don't even know your name!' he called to the night.

In despair he climbed down.

'Women, eh?' said King, zipping up his fly. 'Wan minute they cannae
get enough o'ye, the next they're diving oot the windae sideways.' He clapped
Harry on the shoulder without washing his hands. 'Take my advice, lad.
There's plenty mair where that wan came fae.'

Bruised, filthy, and back in her everyday clothes, Ella made her way to
where the big, pink limo was parked.

The chauffeur was beckoning her to hurry up and pointing at his watch.

She ran towards the open door . . . but as she dived towards it, it shrank
away from her and she landed in a puddle next to a courgette and a spider.

She sniffled and wept, knowing that a long walk home followed by a
difficult climb in through her bedroom window lay ahead. She was only
wearing one shoe, which by this time had turned back into a manky, pink
£5 trainer.

She was wet. She was muddy. She was exhausted. She was in love with
someone she would probably never see again.

As far as she knew, her dream was over.

CHAPTER 11

Red found life with the Wolf to be not just tolerable, but pleasant. Life had never been like that for her before.

He made, as far as Red was concerned, the best teacher ever, teaching as much or as little as she wanted, as and when she wanted. It struck her as strange that she wanted to learn now, having been such a persistent truant before. When education was forced upon her, she had avoided it. Now that it was simply there for her when she craved it, she found she craved it a lot.

So she could eat as much or as little as she pleased of whatever she pleased. She could come and go as she pleased. She could swim in the surprisingly warm water of the Wolf's fountain. She could watch whatever she liked on television, whenever she wanted. She could learn as much or as little as she liked about almost anything, for the Wolf was very knowledgeable. She was free.

Still all was not perfect. There was still that mysterious promise she would have to fulfill looming over her. There were still the nightmares. And she felt very uncomfortable when she learned that the Wolf dragged homeless people down to force them to do his chores at toothpoint.

'Don't look so shocked,' said the Wolf. 'I am the Big, Bad, Wolf after all. And in any event, I seldom actually have to carry out my threat: most people choose to cooperate.'

'But that's like slavery and that!'

'Hardly,' replied the Wolf. 'I let them go after they've done a few simple tasks. Slavery is full-time. This is more . . . labour-robbery.' He chuckled. 'Come now, Scarlet, are you telling me you've never stolen anything?'

'Aye, but . . . but . . .'

The Wolf sat on the sofa next to her, his elbow slung over the back and his feet up on a golden coffee table. He sat quite as a human would.

'Let me explain my philosophy to you, as plainly as I can,' said the Wolf. 'Suppose I were to tell you that somewhere, thousands of miles away, a child your age was killed in one of your human world's many war zones. Would you feel upset about that?'

She shrugged. 'Suppose so.'

'You don't sound too sure. I suppose the question is . . . would you lose any sleep over it?'

She shrugged.

'No, of course you wouldn't. Why would you? Why should you? You'd feel a pang of sorrow . . . then forget about it.'

'Aye. So?'

'Now suppose I were to bring the tragedy a bit closer. Suppose a car accident on the M8 wiped out an entire family? No one you know. How would you feel about that?'

She shrugged.

'Would it bother you more than the distant death in a distant war in a country you couldn't point to on a map?'

'I suppose.'

'Why? Because it happened to Scottish people? Or because there's more chance that you know someone who knows someone who actually saw it happen?'

She shrugged again.

'Suppose I told you that someone killed themselves earlier today directly above the spot where you are sitting.'

Red stood up and moved to another seat. 'I don't think that's very funny.'

The Wolf cackled. 'No, but your reaction is. Do you think that moving a few feet further away from the event changes the reality of it?'

She crossed her arms, frowned and shrugged. She didn't understand what the Wolf was driving at, and was reluctant to risk making a fool of herself by saying anything.

'In any event, you can relax: I made it up.'

Red did seem to relax a little, uncrossing her arms and breathing a sigh of relief.

'Why are you relieved?'

Red shrugged, but the Wolf's continued silence told her he expected an answer.

''Cause that person didnae die.'

'So what?' said the Wolf. 'You don't know who I was or wasn't talking about. Somebody somewhere is bound to have killed themselves. So why does it bother you if I was telling the truth or not?'

'I don't see what you're getting at.'

'Tell me, Red, are you a vegetarian?'

'No!' she cried. She stretched the word over two syllables, seeming almost offended by the suggestion.

'I thought not.' He gave her a sly, toothy grin. 'But I wonder if you'd enjoy a chicken nugget quite so much if you actually saw the poor bird die?'

She cringed at the thought.

'You see, my dear, human beings are by far the strangest creatures on the planet. You love to think that you're so moral, so decent, so ... *nice* ... that you don't want anything bad to happen to any living thing. The reality is that you just don't want to see it, think about it or be told about it.'

Red's eyebrows knitted together in thought. Her brain was aching because she had never been asked to think about or argue about these things before. She was finding it difficult to think of an argument against what the Wolf was saying, even though she knew in her heart he was wrong.

'Aye, but . . . see if ye got all, like, upset and that every time someone dies anywhere in the world anywhere . . . well, ye'd go mental!'

The Wolf laughed. 'You, my dear, are considerably smarter than you look. You're right, of course. It is impossible to care about everyone, though humans like to pretend to. Which leaves us with a simple choice: to be a monster or to be a hypocrite. Being a noble sort, I choose monster.'

'I . . . still don't quite understand.' *What ye on aboot?* she would have said to anyone she didn't fear.

The Wolf laughed softly. 'Maybe I shouldn't expect you to, but I'll tell you what . . . you can do as many or as few of my everyday household chores as you please, because you are free. But the more you do . . . the less my *borrowees* have to do. If you really care about such thoroughly anonymous people, I daresay you can scrub the odd floor for them?'

In time, Red actually grew to like doing the Wolf's chores. It made her feel worthwhile for the first time in her life.

She was not entirely happy, though. Every so often she felt an unpleasant pang of something close to guilt. A little voice inside her that said she had done wrong and was doing wrong. She could silence the voice by reminding it that she was simply born bad, as her granny had been so fond of telling her. She didn't like herself, but she had long since accepted herself as a bad person.

She told the Wolf about the nightmares once, and he said, 'Now, listen closely, Scarlet. Those nightmares are being given to you by your conscience, and the conscience serves no useful purpose whatsoever. Your conscience will make your life a living hell if you let it. Your conscience will always hold you back. It hates your freedom.'

'I cannae make the nightmares stop,' said Red.

'They'll stop,' said the Wolf. 'You're growing up, dear child. The more time we spend together, the more adept you will become at resisting your bothersome conscience. Trust me . . . one day the nightmares will stop.'

* * *

'The press are still speculating aboot Harry Charming's mystery woman,' King told his mirror from behind his newspaper. 'Apparently it's affecting his performance. Celtic coach is dead worried. He cannae get the woman oot his heid! Pathetic if you ask me.'

'Indeed, Mr King,' replied the mirror.

'Still, it would be great for ratings if we could reunite them live on the Reggie King show, eh? Who is she, anyway?'

'Didn't you recognise her, Mr King?'

'No,' King droned impatiently. 'That's why I asked.'

'The belle of the ball on that fateful evening,' said the mirror, 'was none other than that McCinder wimp.'

'Surely not,' frowned King. 'That . . . gorgeous woman in the stunning dress? But wee Ella's . . . well, wee . . . and a bit . . . rodent-like; feart o' everything.'

'I understand she was treated to a free makeover; attitude as well as clothes. She's not a wee girl anymore.'

'No. Far from it.'

'In any event, I'm afraid getting her on the show is out of the question –'

'So she was winding me up, then? Aboot no recognising me and no fancying me and that?' A boyish grin was beginning to spread across King's face.

'Mr King, if that's the sort of thing that can make or break your day, have you considered that there might be something missing from your life?'

King shot the mirror a poisonous look. 'The only thing missing in my life . . . is a magic mirror who is any use to me whatsoever!'

'I'm hurt, Mr King.'

'Didnae know you could be.'

'Well, I do hope you're prepared to eat those words, Mr King. Because I've broken through your ex's cloaking spell.'

It took a moment for that to sink through King's thick skull. When it did, he leapt into the air and let out a roar of triumph. 'Yes! Oh, yes! I shall be the bonniest man in Glasgow once more! The bonniest man in the Greater Glasgow area! The bonniest man in Scotland! Maybe even the bonniest man in the *Universe!* He leapt forward and kissed the mirror. 'You're brilliant!'

'Thank you,' said the mirror. 'Now would you be so kind as to wipe your smacker-prints off me? That is a bit disgusting.'

King skooshed his only friend with Windowlene and wiped it clean. 'So . . . what's the plan?'

'Later in the day,' said the mirror, 'I will direct you to the exact spot where the annoyingly beautiful Snowy is hiding. What you do to him is up to you.'

One day, the Wolf said to Red, 'Do you remember . . . it must seem like a long time ago now . . . you promised to do me a favour?'

Red's heart skipped a beat, but she tried not to show it. 'Hmm?'

'There are three little pigs,' said the Wolf. His features darkened and he pointed to the patches of missing fur and burnt flesh. 'They did this to me!'

'I'm sorry,' said Red, for want of anything better to say.

'Oh, I don't want sympathy,' said the Wolf. 'I want revenge.'

She gulped. 'What can I do?'

'Simple,' said the Wolf. 'I will give you a knife. You will go to the brick house where the three little pigs live. You will say that you have run away from home, that you have heard of the famous pigs' hospitality, and wondered if they would give you a bite to eat.

'They are stupid, so they will invite you in and tell you to make your-self at home. They will feed you and put you up for the night. I want you to kill them as they sleep.'

'I cannae dae that!' gasped Red.

'You promised, Scarlet. You cannot break a promise, especially not after everything I've done for you.'

Red felt dizzy. All she wanted at that moment was to be home; her real home, with her abusive grandmother, who was all the family she had.

But that home didn't exist anymore. That life wasn't hers to live. She had murdered her gran, moved in with the Wolf, and nothing could ever go back to the way it was. She was trapped.

'It's . . . it's evil,' she stammered.

'Oh, come, now, child. Have I taught you nothing? Good and evil are abstract human ideas that don't have any real meaning.' He sighed. 'Do you know what an MSH certificate is?'

Red shrugged.

'MSH stands for Minimum Standard of Humanity. You see, most people think that in Europe, animals with the power of speech have human rights automatically. Utter balderdash! What about parrots?'

'So?'

'To get human rights, an animal with the power of speech must sit a test. To make sure they have the *Minimum Standard of Humanity*. Then they get the certificate that lets them get certain basic human rights. Now, isn't it funny that it's not called Minimum Standard of Goodness or Minimum Standard of Worthiness, or even Minimum Standard of Non-Evil? No. What is required is a Minimum Standard of *Humanity*. Stop me if I'm going too fast for you . . .'

'Naw, it's fine.'

'Now, the test looks for several things to see how human-ish the animal has become. Can they understand complicated ideas? Can they use their imagination? Can they resist their animal instincts? In other words, most humans would fail. But a human being doesn't have to pass a test to get human rights. A human being just has to be born. So where's the equality?'

Red shrugged. She was finding it harder and harder to pretend she knew what the Wolf was on about.

'One of the things they test you on,' the Wolf went on, 'is moral accountability. Do you know what "moral accountability" means?'

'Like, right and wrang and that?' shrugged Red.

'Indeed, the concept of right and wrong. Also, your understanding of the importance of choosing right, and the consequences of choosing wrong, you see?'

Red shrugged. 'So?'

'So, I have an MSH certificate. I passed their little test because I understand moral accountability. I understand it . . . I just don't agree with it.

'Throughout history, human beings have been very, very nasty to creatures and people who aren't like them: different races, different sexes, different species, whatever. "Right" has always meant being nice to "us" and nasty to "them"; "them" being everyone else. But slowly people have grown to accept the whole human race as "us". Some people have. Others remain convinced that their own race, religion, gender, whatever, is superior to all the others. But still animals don't count. It is considered less wrong to harm an animal than to harm a person, is it not?'

His deep gaze bore into her and she shifted uncomfortably, aware that she had to give some sort of an answer. 'Depends,' she shrugged.

The wolf laughed his deadly yet gentle laugh. 'Yes, indeed. I think you'll find that everything always "depends".

'Look after your own kind, Scarlet. That is the only morality that has ever truly existed. Do you understand?'

'Yes,' she said, and she did . . . but she didn't want to.

'It's the same in nature. The cat doesn't feel compassion for the bird it eats. The bird doesn't feel compassion for the spider. The spider doesn't feel compassion for the fly. You don't feel compassion for the cow your double cheeseburger used to be. That cow never felt compassion for a blade of grass. Every living thing only cares about its own kind. That's the way it should be. It's natural.'

'Aye,' said Red, trying to puzzle out what she was supposed to make of all this. 'But, um . . . so what?'

'Scarlet, my dear, you are looking at the only known MSH wolf. It is a very lonely existence, but one I have become used to. When I take care of my own, I take care of just myself, because I am the only one. Everything

I own, everything I have achieved is down to looking after Number One, and doing terrible things to anyone who gets in my way.' He pointed to his wounds once more, and all trace of gentleness left his voice when he growled, 'THEY DID THIS TO ME! I can't have that, they must pay. If I don't take my revenge, with your help, my reputation will be ruined and I will have nothing. Which means you will have nothing.'

'I understand,' said Red, trembling, 'but I'm still no daeing it.'

'Scarlet, let me put it to you another way,' said the Wolf, turning on his gentle, charming voice once more. 'You (a human) asked me (a wolf) to kill your grandmother (a human. A blood relative, no less!). I (a wolf) am asking you (a human) to kill some pigs. I've never killed my own kind, so which of us is truly evil?'

'You're right,' said Red, nodding bitterly. 'I am eviller than you. But the best I can dae is no get any worse.'

'My dear Scarlet, do you really think I planned on giving you a choice? I hate to do this to you, but whenever I eat someone, I always leave part of them – an arm or a leg, usually – just in case I need to . . . persuade someone to follow my advice.'

Red clapped a hand over her mouth.

'I see you understand me. I can arrange for the police to find evidence that you alone killed your grandmother and you will spend the best years of your life behind bars. Or you can spend them with me, living in luxury and comfort. You can be free, Scarlet.'

'I don't deserve to be free.'

The Wolf chuckled. 'Deserving or not deserving . . . another human concept that doesn't mean very much. Forget what you deserve and do what you want. If you want to go to jail, I will put you there, and find someone else to be my friend. If you don't want to go to jail, do exactly as I say.'

CHAPTER 12

'I think I'm going to like it here,' Rapunzel said of her luxury home, throwing herself backwards onto the sofa.

'Me, too!' squealed Upenda, turning a cartwheel across the living room floor.

'Glad you like it,' said Jack, snuggling beside Rapunzel. 'Everything's going to be alright now.'

Rapunzel got a faraway look in her eyes. 'I hope so, Jack,' she said, softly. 'I really do.'

Her manner worried Jack. She was his wife-to-be, yet there was so much he didn't know about her, so much pain inside her he couldn't make better.

Finally, he asked what he knew she didn't want him to, but he had wanted to for so long: 'Punzy, why did you leave your country?'

She sat upright and shrugged him off. 'I cannot tell you. Jack, I cannot. There is too much shame.'

'Och, just tell him, Mum,' said Upenda. 'It's really no that big a deal.'

'Upenda knows and I don't?' said Jack, trying not to pout.

'It is nothing to do with you,' Rapunzel insisted.

Upenda turned suddenly grave. 'He's back, Mum. You were afraid he might find us, you hoped he wouldnae . . . well he has. He came to me when I was in care. I didnae want to tell you . . . but don't you tell me it's nothing to do wi' me, because it's everything to do wi' me. And Jack needs to know.'

Rapunzel was trembling. 'You promised you'd tell me immediately if you saw him.'

'I didnae want you to be like you are now.'

'Knowing his name will not protect you forever. I need to know at once if he is near!'

'Who?' demanded Jack. 'Who are you talking aboot?'

Rapunzel squeezed her eyes shut and began her story.

'When I was quite young, my father had a friend whose daughter was cleverer, prettier and better at sports than me. He used to come home drunk and beg me to be good at something. I would cry myself to sleep, as I believed I was good at nothing. I said, "But father, my hair is twice as long as my body. Is that not wonderful? Does that not make me special?" He flew into a rage and cut it all off. But it grew back even longer.

'When my father died, I thought I was a horrible person because even though I was sad, a part of me was a little bit relieved. And I swore that I would never again let anyone cut my hair.

'My father could not be proud of me as I was, so he lied about me, so he could pretend to be proud. He said that I could spin straw into gold.

'The King of my country came to hear of this, and for some reason he came to believe it.

'He said he would marry me. My father was pleased, as we were poor, but I was not pleased, as the King was ugly and smelled strange. I had no choice.

'I was less pleased still when I found out that he believed I could spin straw into gold, and would chop my head off if I did not.

'He locked me in a cellar filled with straw and a spinning wheel, and told me he expected it all turned to gold by morning or I would die.

'I was hysterical. I cried and cried.

'A hooded figure appeared to me and asked me why I was crying. He said he could help me but there would be a price. I said, "But I have nothing." He said that I could give him a child. So I agreed, and he spun the straw into gold, and I bore him a child, and the king did not execute me.

[114]

'I came to love the child growing inside me, and I knew I could not let this creature take it away from me forever, but I knew no way to stop him.

'So I went to the library and I read and I read, and I found out that the creature was a Dark Elf and that guessing a Dark Elf's name gave you power over him. I also discovered that if you challenge him to the name game, he is powerless for three days while you try to guess his name.

'When the creature came for my newborn baby, I challenged him, but that meant the King now knew he was not Upenda's true father. He ordered us both killed. I had to flee. I spent the next three days trying desperately to find someone, somewhere, who knew of some clue to the creature's name . . . yet I knew I had to stay out of reach of the King. It was difficult. On the first and second days, he came to me and taunted me:"Have you guessed my name, yet? Have you guessed my name yet?"

'On the third day, I had all but given up hope, when I came to a clearing, where I saw a sight I will never forget.

'The creature was playing football with a severed head. There were two trees he was using for goalposts . . . he volleyed the head between the two, and ran around celebrating and singing,"There's only one Rumpelstiltskin." That is how I knew.

'So when he came for the child, he sneered at me and said,"I'm here for my child . . . unless, of course, you know my name?"

'I clutched my child tightly to me and said, "Your name is Rumpelstiltskin!"

'He screamed and vanished in a great ball of fire. I hoped he was dead, but knew he was probably not.

'I managed to escape the country and found an agent who could help me get to Britain. And here I am.

'If he has returned, I do not want to say his name too often. It has less power every time it is used, and it won't protect us forever.'

Jack was silent.

Upenda, who had heard this story before, had become more interested in her Gameboy.

The ostrich (whom Jack had named Baxter) was trying to offer some comfort to Rapunzel by nuzzling her.

Finally, Jack said, 'I promise I will do whatever it takes to keep you and your daughter safe. I'm King of the Beanstalk, remember? I can protect you.'

'Except the polis confiscated yer magic sword,' Upenda remarked nonchalantly.

'Aye, well,' said Jack, 'I might just have a wee secret aboot that.' He held his hands high above his head, cried 'Sword!' and the sword appeared in his hand, flames leaping from its blade. 'Return,' he said, and it vanished. 'See? The polis are just looking after it for me. I can get it when I need it.'

'Anyone want to hear my story?' Thumbelina called from her doll's house.

No one replied. So she went on with the story anyway.

'It all started wi' my maw, who wanted mair than anything to have a wean, but the doctor says she couldnae.

'So she goes to a good witch, and she gies her a daud o' magic barley and says "Here, plant that".

'So my maw's away hame wi' this daud o' barley, and she's like that: "A wee daud o' barley? What's that supposed to dae?".

'But she takes it hame and she plants it, and the next day she wakes up, and there's this pure weird purple flower growing oot the plant pot. And its petals is a' closed.

'So she gies it a kiss, and the flower opens, and there's me! That's how I got born!'

'Great story, Thumbsy,' said Jack.

'I'm no finished!' snapped Thumbelina. 'Noo, where was I? Oh, aye, getting born.

'Noo, she called me Thumbelina, because I was the size of her man's thumb, and I never grew any bigger.

'She took me to see the witch, to say thanks for getting born and that, and the witch is like that to me: "You're destined to marry the King o' the Pixies, by the way!" So that's how I know.

[116]

'Have I tellt yous I'm destined to marry the King o' the Pixies?

'Anyway, I was happy, until wan day, this big, fat, slimy frog jumps in the windae and snatches me away!

'Turns oot she wants me to marry her son, who's an even fatter, slimier frog!

'So I'm like that: "No way am I marrying a frog! I'm destined to marry the King o' the Pixies." Besides, frogs is slimy and smelly and horrible. Nae offence or that.

'But, see, they werenae for giving me a choice, and they stranded me on a lily pad in the middle o' the lake, so's I couldnae escape.

'See me, though? I might be wee, but I've got a big brain. I knew there was no way I could swim all the way to the banks o' the pond, but I could swim under the lily pad. Underwater, I wrapped my belt around the stalk and pulled it tight, and the belt cut through the stalk and it broke off, like I thought. Then I climbed back on and I had a wee boat!

'I chucked my belt to a passing bat, who gied us a wee pull. It was dead good of him. The wind blew my hair every which way! It was just like waterskiing!

'Anyways, that's how I got to dry land, and I started trying to make my way hame, but I was lost.

'Then the weather took a turn for the worse, which is a right scary thing if you're wee enough to droon in a puddle! As I wandered aboot helplessly looking for the way home, I was aye getting laughed at by animals who'd never seen a human being sae wee, but it never got to me. I kept telling mysel', "I'm destined to marry the King o' the Pixies! I'm destined to marry the King o' the Pixies!" And that's what kept me going.

'Eventually I comes to this cottage and knocks on the door. I was desperate for a wee bit meal and somewhere to stay, and somewhere to dry my claithes. It was a wee field mouse that lived there, and he was like that: "Och, what ye daeing oot there in that?" He took me in and got me all warm and dry. He was dead good to me, that wee moose.

'The moose's pal, the mole, came round to visit, and he's dead posh and that . . . of course, he falls madly in love wi' me and wants to marry me!

'I tried to tell him I was destined to marry the King o' the Pixies, but he was having nane o' it, and finally I started thinking . . . maybe I wasnae gonnae find the King o' the Pixies. Maybe I couldnae dae any better than this mole.

'Then wan day I was on my way to his bit, through a' the tunnels and that, and what does I see in the tunnel? A hauf-deid bird.

'So I'm for helping it, and the mole's like that: "Why should we? It's his ain fault for messing aboot in the sky instead o' getting underground like me."

'Well, I was just speechless! I goes like that to him: "See you? You're a cold-hearted misery-guts, and I wouldnae marry you if you *were* the King o' the Pixies!"

'So that was that then. I took the poor bird back to the moose's hoose, and nursed it back to health. Me and the bird became great friends, and when it could fly again, it took me on its back. I'd nae idea how to get hame, or where to look for the King o' the Pixies, so we just kept looking . . . till the giant caught us.

'I bit his hand hard enough to make him let the bird go. I shouts, "Don't mind me, you just run!"

'Then the giant takes me to his castle and locks me in a cage. Every time he goes oot hunting, I start screaming for help, and that's where you came in. How we got up the beanstalk is anybody's guess . . . must be some sort of gateway between your world and mine.

'Anyways, that's my heroic story.'

She took a bow.

'Gaun yersel', Thumbsy,' said Jack, in an uninterested tone. Then he excused himself, as he'd been desperate to do for most of Thumbelina's account.

* * *

[118]

Snowy, too, was called upon to tell a story. The story of how he had come down from the Highlands, fallen in love and been whisked away into a world of madness and danger.

But he was sick of telling it.

'Tell you what,' he said to the Freaks, who were tucked in, eagerly awaiting their bedtime story. 'You've heard my story almost every night since I arrived here . . . but I haven't heard yours even once. Tell me your story.'

'What do you mean, tell you oor story?' snapped Crabbit. 'Nae idea what you're talking aboot!'

'Your story, Crabbit. Like I told you mine. You know . . . Who you are, and – no offence – *what* you are, and where you come from, and how you know Jill, and why you're hiding in this house that doesn't exist . . . That's your story.'

Crabbit yawned loudly. 'Well, I think we need an early night the night. Nice talking to ye and that.'

'No story?' whimpered Glaikit.

'Story!' growled Dagger.

'Crabbit,' Dragonman spoke up, softly, 'I think we should tell him. He deserves to know and cannae harm us with the knowledge.'

Crabbit sighed. 'Alright, then. What we are, Dandruff, is an aberration! An affront to everything decent and natural! In other words . . . we're freaks.

'It all started in the lab of one Doctor Demenscient; the sort o' scientist who thinks anything that adds to human knowledge is worth daeing, whatever the cost. He created his experiment by . . . I don't even know what he done. Take a lump o' human tissue, clone it to something almost human, make it mutate, expose it to all sorts of radiation, electrical currents, graft in some microchips, mix in some animal DNA, plant DNA, broon sauce . . . I don't know. Whatever he done, something horrible came oot o' it. Whatever he intended to create . . . it wasnae us!

'There were thirty experiments in all. You're talking to the last remaining five. You see, when he realised he was getting into trouble wi' the Bioethics Commission, he decided to destroy the evidence. We were only weans, but

[119]

we escaped. Since then, we've stuck together like glue, you know? We're family. Anyone messes wi' wan of us messes wi' all of us.

'So we roamed the land trying to find human beings who wouldn't mock us or attack us or run away screaming or call the polis or try and set fire to us. You'd be surprised how intolerant people can be.

'We only found wan human who was willing to value us for who we were, to treat us wi' a wee bit dignity and help us oot. That was Jill.

'Doctor Demenscient was still after us, though, so we had to go into hiding. We built this place. Jill made it safe for us wi' the magic, and we've been here ever since. The end.'

'Wow,' said Snowy, who found it hard to take in a story so extraordinary. 'So you can't leave this place until Doctor Demenscient dies?'

Crabbit laughed out loud. 'He died over a year ago. We had a big party when we heard. We're still here because we like it here, Snowy.'

'You see,' Dragonman piped in. 'We have grown accustomed to our way of life here. We are self-sufficient. We have everything we need right here. We grow our own food. We keep up with the outside world – from a safe distance, mind you – through the television. The outside world need never know we exist, and we need never particularly care that it exists. It's our own little Garden of Eden.'

'Can we hear the story aboot the guy fae the high fields noo?' asked Glaikit.

'High fields?' asked Snowy, confused.

'I think he means "Highlands",' Crabbit explained.

'Oh.' Snowy chuckled. 'The guy from the Highlands is me, Glaikit. I'm the guy from the Highlands.'

Glaikit laughed. 'Don't be silly! You're no in a story! You're real!'

Snowy sighed and told his story again. Then he climbed downstairs to bed, not knowing it would be his last night in the Freaks' house.

CHAPTER 13

'Harry, I'm taking you off for the second half.'

The Celtic manager's tone left no room for argument.

Harry argued anyway: 'But . . . but . . . how are ye subbing me off for?'

He mopped his sweat-soaked brow, frustrated.

'Because you keep missing sitters, getting mugged for the ball, and yer delivery is woeful. When you're on form, Harry, there's no doubt you're the best player in Scotland. But right at the moment, you're playing a lot of mince.'

'But . . . but . . .'

'Don't you "But-but" me, Son. Wee piece of advice for you . . . whatever's distracting you, get it dealt wi'. Everyone knows what's distracting you. You got the shoe with you?'

'Aye,' said Harry. 'Always kiss it afore a match, for luck.'

'Fat lot o' good that's been doing ye. Gie's a look.'

Obediently, Harry fetched the sparkling shoe from his locker.

'See that? The woman that wears that has quite small feet. I reckon if you went through the guest list from your party, found each and every woman that was there and ask them to try it on, there wouldnae be many it'd fit.'

The boss drew a deep breath and clapped Harry on the shoulder. 'Find her. Whatever it takes, I want you – I'm ordering you – to get out there and find her. If you need to hire private detectives or anything, we'll pay for it, because when you're on form, it'd cost more to bring in a player a tenth as good to replace you. But the way you're playing the noo . . . you're gonnae end up replaced. And you'll be lucky to end up at Queen of the South. Find her!'

Thunder roared and lightning flashed, and the wind screamed as it sent horizontal rain into Wee Red Hoodie's face. She felt as if she were wading up some angry river against the current, and her red hoodie was turned maroon with water.

She was so cold, so wet and so afraid as she made her weary way, one heavy, squelching step at a time, to the three wee pigs' front door.

She held her breath, shaking all over, as much from cold as from fear. She knocked the door.

She saw a pig open the door. A pig she would kill. All at once, she forgot what she had been told to say. 'I, um . . . I . . .' Her voice failed her. Her heart failed her. She just cried.

'Och, come on in, Hen,' said Paddy Pig, beckoning her into the reassuring warmth of the brick house, and moving a chair for her to sit in front of the blazing fire.

She sat down gratefully as the pigs brought her a towel and a bowl of steaming hot spicy vegetable soup.

The pigs had a pleasant little cottage, with plain white walls. The only real decoration was a poster with the Burns poem, 'To a Mouse' in big, white letters. She'd never read Burns and certainly couldn't understand him, but she became fixated with it between mouthfuls of soup. It was that or look the pigs in the eye.

'There,' said Paddy. 'Get some o' that doon ye. Ye'll feel better in nae time.'

'Thanks,' Red whispered, sipping the soup guiltily.

'Nae bother at all,' said Paddy. 'Look at the state of ye! Poor thing. Ye're soaked through!'

'Aye, I am that.'

'Percy,' said Peter, 'away doon to the basement, see if ye cannae find her anything dry to wear.'

'Och,' said Percy, stomping huffily off. 'Yous make me dae everything!'

Paddy laughed. 'He'll be up in a minute wi' some dry claithes. So, tell me, Hen, what were ye daeing oot there in that?'

'Long story,' murmured Red, slurping her soup.

'Fair enough,' said Paddy. 'Ye got a name, or dae we have to keep calling you "Hen"?'

'Scarlet. Scarlet Hood. My pals a' call me Red, though, or Wee Red Hoodie.'

'Red it is, then,' said Paddy, with a friendly snort.

Percy returned and tossed some dry clothes her way. 'Sorry, this is all I could find. Pigs don't usually wear claithes.'

Red nodded gratefully and headed to the bathroom. She returned presently wearing a T-shirt bearing the image of Miss Piggy and the slogan *Kermit's a dafty!* and a kilt.

'That,' said Paddy with pride, pointing to the kilt, 'is Porcine Tartan. You're probably not aware of this, but us pigs are in fact the only MSH animal group to have our own official tartan.'

The other pigs beamed with pride.

'That's interesting,' said Red, who found it boring.

'Aye,' said Peter. 'There's a lot to be proud of in being a pig.'

'So what brings ye to our door?' asked Percy.

Red shrunk into her seat and shrugged.

'She doesnae have to tell us if she doesnae want to,' growled Paddy, giving his youngest brother a warning glare.

'Aye,' said Percy, 'but I really want to know.'

'It was my gran,' said Red. 'I . . . was staying wi' her since my maw and da died. Got fed up wi' getting knocked aboot affae her, so I ran away. Didnae know where to go. Somebody says, find some pigs, they'll look after ye. So here I am.'

'They gied ye good advice,' said Peter. 'We're aye happy to take in a stray. Right, Paddy?'

'Aye, well said, Peter,' replied Paddy, 'very well said indeed. See us pigs, Red? We're a' that's good aboot Glasgow. Ye'll notice that every time this city gets into the headlines for the wrong reasons, it's aye humans that's behind it. Well that's no how it is wi' us pigs. We'll take anybody in. Treat anybody like a brother or sister. It's important to us, see?'

'Aye,' said Peter. 'Unless ye mess wi' us. Then ye get seen to. Like that Wolf guy.'

'Aye,' said Percy, bouncing with enthusiasm. 'Tell her the story aboot the Wolf.'

Paddy told the story complete with guffaws and roars of approval from his brothers.

'Do you no think yous were a bit harsh?' said Red. 'I mean, like . . . even though what the Wolf done was bad and that . . . cooking him was a bit much, was it no?'

Silence fell, and grew increasingly awkward as it lingered.

'Takes a lot o' guts to say what you just said,' Paddy told her slowly. 'I respect that. You're a really good kid and I like you a lot, but what ye have to understand aboot the Wolf is . . . he was that angry at no being able to blow oor hoose doon, he'd've had us for breakfast. No doubt about it. We had nae choice, see?'

'Aye,' said Red.

'We don't dae stuff like that very often,' Paddy went on. 'Maist o' the time, we wouldnae say "boo" to a goose!'

'Hey, you know what?' said Percy. 'I reckon a new addition to the family would be a great excuse for a party.'

'True,' said Peter. 'That's another thing ye'll learn aboot pigs, Red. We'll never pass up an excuse for a party!'

'Very well spoken,' said Paddy. 'And she is wearing Pig Tartan and the sacred T-shirt. What do you say, Red? Fancy being an honorary pig?'

Red didn't quite know what to say to that. She shrugged coyly and muttered, 'Aye, awright then.'

'Then I solemnly hereby confer upon you the sacred honour and that, of honorary pighood.'

'Is it no piggery?' asked Percy.

'Shut it, you!' snapped Paddy. 'Red, do you accept?'

'Aye,' Red replied, a tear in her eye.

'Well, that's it, then,' said Paddy. 'You're a pig!'

His brothers cheered and wheezed and grunted, clapping Red on the shoulder and hugging her with their trotters. Then they burst into song:

> Hello! Hello!
> We are the Three Wee Pigs!

'Four Wee Pigs,' Paddy corrected.

> Hello! Hello!
> We are the Four Wee Pigs!

When they started singing, 'If you're proud to be a grumphie, clap yer trotters,' Red joined in, laughing and clapping her hands.

When they sang. 'Stand up if ya hate the Wolf!' she leapt to her feet with gusto.

She felt warm and welcome. She felt cherished. The pigs had taken her in, just as the Wolf had . . . but the Wolf was using her. The hospitality of the pigs was coming straight from their wee hearts.

She began to wonder if she could bring herself to do what she had come to do. Every time that thought arose, she growled inwardly at her conscience and remembered all the advice of the Wolf.

She also avoided looking at the pigs by staring at the poem on the wall.

Wee, sleekit, cow'rin, tim'rous beastie,
O, what a panic's in thy breastie!
Thou need na start awa sae hasty,
Wi' bickering brattle!
I wad be laith to rin an' chase thee,
Wi' murd'ring pattle!

'Ye a fan o' Burns?' Paddy asked her suddenly. He had spotted her gaze.

'Naw, no really,' said Red, blushing. She didn't really want to admit that she didn't understand what she was reading.

'That's only up there because Paddy thinks it's funny,' said Peter with a glare.

'Well, it is funny,' chuckled Paddy.

Red pretended to smile, though she didn't really get the joke.

'See, the wee moose in the poem got its hoose wrecked,' said Peter. 'Just like me and Percy did.'

'Because ye never followed my advice,' said Paddy. 'That poem's up there to remind yous o' that!'

Percy seemed to recognise that Red didn't understand the poem, and didn't want to say. 'See, Rabbie Burns was oot ploughing the field one day . . . and he accidentally wrecked a wee moose's nest. So he wrote the poem 'To a Mouse', which says to the mouse . . . "Sorry aboot that, mate. Didnae mean it."'

'It's no just saying sorry, though,' said Peter. 'It's also saying "I know how ye feel." Burns identified wi' the mouse, because he knew what it was like to have everything he worked so hard for wrecked in an instant.'

'Aye,' said Paddy. 'But if the moose had built a brick hoose, maybe he'd've wrote a poem aboot breaking his plough.'

'Shut it, you!' snapped Percy.

Peter ignored them both and quoted:

But, Mousie, thou art no thy lane,
In proving foresight may be vain;
The best laid schemes o' mice an' men
Gang aft agley,
An' lea'e us nought but grief an' pain,
For promis'd joy!

Tears were now running down Red's face.

'What is it?' asked Paddy.

'He had compassion,' sniffled Red. She found it hard to talk past her choking tears. 'He was a man ... and he felt compassion for a wee moose.' She took a deep breath, clenched her teeth and made the biggest decision of her life. 'There's something yous need to know. See the Big, Bad Wolf? He's still after ye. He sent me to murder yous all!'

'What?' roared Paddy.

Bright lights shone through the window. They heard the roar of a monstrous engine nearby. The pigs looked out the window and, to their horror, saw a bulldozer trundling towards their house, and could make out a hairy silhouette within.

For the Big, Bad Wolf had not been entirely relying on the loyalty of Red: he had a Plan B. A small listening device sat on the outside windowsill, and the enemy of the pigs had heard every sound they made.

'Traitor!' Paddy roared at Red. 'We took you in, treated you like wan o' us!'

The other pigs snorted hatefully at her.

'I'm sorry!' she wailed.

Confusion reigned as the pigs darted desperately about.

'Grab some stuff,' called Paddy. 'Anything we don't need, don't grab it. We're leaving!'

'What aboot her?' said Percy. 'Do we lock her in and let her get buried?'

'Naw,' said Paddy. 'It'd harm us mair than her to become killers.' But he spat in her face for good measure.

[127]

The pigs escaped just before their house was razed to the ground. Their brick house. Their pride and joy. Their home, their life and their dream.

But they had no time to grieve. The wolf was bearing down upon them hard and fast, the wicked glint in his eye made all the more menacing by his burned flesh and missing fur. Only murder was on his vengeful mind.

They ran as one. They knew that if they spread out, it would be likely that two of them would survive. But that's not how pigs do things.

Suddenly, Wee Red Hoodie jumped on the back of the wolf, grabbing at his ears, biting at the burnt flesh where his fur was thinnest, and making him tumble to the ground.

By the time the Wolf had shaken off the girl, the pigs were nowhere to be seen.

He snarled at the child, and my! What big teeth he had!

'Have you completely lost your mind?'

'Naw,' said Red. 'I've found it.'

'My dear child, you do know you're going to die, don't you?'

'I deserve to die!' she screamed. 'But what I just done for them wee pigs . . . that might just keep me oot o' Hell!'

'Good luck with that,' said the Wolf.

And in the next instant, Wee Red Hoodie was no more.

CHAPTER 14

'Och, leave him sleeping,' whispered Crabbit over the snoring form of Snowy White. 'He seems to need it mair than we do.'

Though it was still early evening, Snowy was napping when the freaks went out to collect firewood.

Snowy woke to find himself staring into the face of an ugly hag. She bore a passing resemblance to Crabbit, and at first he thought it was she . . . but, no. This hag, despite having an ugly, green, wrinkled face and torn black robes . . . had the most beautiful eyes he had ever seen (apart from Jill's).

'Sssh,' hissed the hag. 'It's okay. I'm the tablet fairy.'

She presented him with a tray full of his favourite, buttery sweet.

'What are you doing here?'

'I visit the worthy while they sleep to offer free tablet!' cried the tablet fairy. 'And you are certainly worthy.'

Snowy's mouth watered at the sweet smell: it smelled just like his mother's. She'd call him in when he'd been out playing and he'd pick up his football and dash in, drooling in anticipation. So many memories in such a simple smell, and he could tell at a glance that the texture was perfect. Still . . .

'How do I know I can trust you?'

'Because if I meant you harm, I could never have got through Jill's cloaking spell.'

Snowy shrugged. That was good enough for him.

He had forgotten all about Crabbit's crystal ball. The one she had told him to keep near him at all times, because it would warn him of approaching danger . . . the one that was burning and glowing furiously, unseen under a pile of laundry on the floor.

He put just a small piece into his mouth, for a nibble at a time is the only proper way to savour the flavour of tablet. Its sweet taste spread over his tongue and pleasantly warmed the back of his throat.

How wonderful he felt for a moment.

Then he felt weak. Not the usual just-woken-up weak; this was another level of weakness that gripped him from deep within and crippled him utterly.

He could smell cough syrup. He was seeing double. The tablet fairy was laughing. Why was she laughing? And why was her laugh so . . . manly?

Though his vision was blurred, he could see she was pulling her face off. He tried to scream, *Don't pull your face off. It's not good for your health at all!*

No words would come out.

Then he saw that she was not pulling her face off at all, it was a mask, and she was not the tablet fairy, she – *he* – was Reginald King, come to finish him off.

'Fool,' he was saying. 'Dae ye no recognise yer nemesis?'

But he sounded so far away.

And then there was darkness.

'Snowy? Snowy?!' Crabbit was shaking him desperately.

He wasn't breathing. She couldn't find his pulse.

Nono's head wasn't spinning, nor was he repeating his usual syllable. Instead he was facing the ceiling, letting out a howl of anguish, like a coyote.

Dagger was swishing his knife-hands through the air at imaginary enemies: he preferred anger to mourning. 'The family creed . . .' he snarled slowly. 'It applies here, yes?'

Tears were falling from Crabbit's grossly misshapen eyes, onto Snowy's body. 'Mess wi' wan of us, mess wi' all of us,' she quoted. 'He came into oor lives. We didnae ask him to, but he came. He made us laugh. He shared his story and listened to oors. He helped wi' the gardening and the cooking and never complained. Somehow or other he became as much wan of us as any of us. Aye, too right the creed applies.'

'We kill King?' roared Dagger, stabbing at the air.

'We don't kill!' snapped Crabbit. 'But by God, we'll take away what he cares aboot the maist!'

Dragonman was calmly sniffing Snowy's mouth. 'Thanatosium,' he diagnosed. 'It's a magical poison preferred by evil faeries. There's a chance.'

'What do you mean a chance? He's deid! Nae breath, nae heartbeat, nae nothing!'

'The victim of Thanatosium succumbs to a death-like state for three days, during which the body, though it shows no signs of life, will not cool or decompose. If the antidote is not given to him within that time, he dies forever.'

'What's the antidote, then?'

'Twee as it sounds . . . true love's kiss.'

A moment's silence came over the room.

'He loves Jill,' said Glaikit, pleased to know something important for once.

'Get her here, now!' commanded Crabbit. Dragonman was already fumbling in Snowy's pockets for his mobile.

'And no a word to her aboot what we're gonnae dae to her ex,' insisted Crabbit. 'She's a big soft lump when it comes to stuff like that. Better we just get on wi' it!'

'I'm no gonnae let ye buy me a hoose, Jack.'

'How no?' asked Jack. He was almost pleading.

'Because . . . ye don't just let folk buy hooses for ye.'

Jack looked around the flat. 'But . . . do ye no want to get oot o' here?'

[131]

'Aye,' said Jill. 'But . . . I want to dae it mysel'. Okay?'

Jack slumped. 'It's just . . . you've done so much for me . . . and Punzy. I want to dae something for you, you know?'

'Och, just leave her,' said a voice from Jack's shirt pocket. 'If she wants to be a numpty and turn doon free hooses, that's her problem.'

'Who asked you?' said Jill, glaring at the offending pocket.

Out popped Thumbelina. 'Naebody ever asks me anything, but I still tell them what I think.'

Jill couldn't help but be irritated with Thumbsy, but only when she talked.

'Maybe naebody asks you anything because naebody wants you to say anything, you annoying little bug. Or do you like annoying people just so's they'll notice ye?'

Thumbelina folded her tiny arms. 'Well, you of all people should know better than to make fun of somebody's size, ya big, fat pig!'

'What did you call me?' gasped Jill.

Thumbelina grinned nastily. Jill felt the blood rushing to her face. It was no secret she was sensitive about her weight.

'Come on, guys,' Jack interjected in his most soothing voice. 'We don't need this.'

Jill glared at Thumbelina, but before either of them could say anything, there was a knock at the door.

Glad of a chance to escape, Jill answered the door . . . and found herself face-to-face with the mother she had not seen in four years.

'Maw!' Jill said, trying not to gape.

'Can I come in?' asked Maw.

'Aye. Aye, of course.'

Maw waddled awkwardly through the door and into the living room. She sat down on the sofa and an awkward silence fell.

'Some weather we've been getting, eh?'

'Aye,' said Jack.

'So how've you been, Maw?' asked Jill, to break the ice.

'No too bad,' said Maw. 'Things awright wi' you?'

'Och, cannae complain.'

'Aye, good, good, aye,' said Maw, trying to call to mind some of the other words she knew. 'Aye. Ye still seeing that celebrity boyfriend o' yours?'

'Naw,' said Jill. 'Me and Reggie broke up a while ago.'

'Och, ye're daft!' said Maw. 'Ye shoulda married his money, then left him!'

'Aye, right enough.'

'Listen, Jill . . . see all this time I've no been in touch . . . I was aye meaning to phone. I just, um . . . didnae.'

'Aye,' said Jill. 'Aye, me too. Listen, can I get ye a cup of tea or that?' asked Jill.

'Aye, that would be lovely. Thanks.'

As soon as Jill had gone through to the kitchen, Maw turned to Jack.

'Listen, Jack, I . . . maybe I shouldnae have says some o' the things I says and that, afore ye left.'

'Naw . . .' Jack agreed.

'Also, I . . . maybe I misjudged whatserface a wee bit.'

Jack's studded eyebrows shot up. 'Whatserface?'

'Aye, you know,' said Maw, gesturing awkwardly. 'You know . . . Rasputin, or whatever it is you call her.'

'Rapunzel, you mean?' Jack asked icily.

'Aye.'

'Well, I don't see how you can judge her or misjudge her,' said Jack. 'You've never met her!'

'Aye, that's true enough.'

'If you want to make it up to me, you'll spend some time wi' her. Get to know her a bit.'

'Aye, awright,' said Maw. 'I'll take her doon the pub the morra night. She can watch the Rangers game wi' me.'

'That's no quite what I –'

Jack didn't manage to finish his sentence before the phone rang and Jill ran in to answer it.

'Hello? . . . What's wrong? . . . Oh, no. Um . . . okay, I'll be there as soon as I can . . . Right. Bye.'

She packed herself into her jacket and said, 'I'm really sorry, I've got to go.'

'Is everything awright?' asked Jack.

'Um . . . sort of. I'm sorry, it's a really long story. I've got to go. Bye.'

Ella was scrubbing a pot when there came a knock at the door.

'Keep her out of sight while I get that,' said her foster father. Kara and Clara ushered her into the conservatory.

'My word,' said their father when he answered the door. 'This is a surprise and an honour.'

Harry Charmaine had his hands in his pockets and was staring at the ground, shifting uncomfortably. 'Um . . . hello.'

Ella could hear every word and recognised Harry's voice instantly. Her heart pounded and her brain roared, but she dared not present herself.

'Can I come in?'

'Please, be my guest. Make yourself at home. Can I get you anything?'

Harry chuckled nervously. 'Um . . . that sort of depends . . .' He lapsed into an embarrassed silence and stared at his feet.

Kara and Clara oozed into the room.

'Harry Charmaine!' beamed Kara. 'It's such an honour!' She grabbed his hand and kissed it.

'Yes, an honour,' echoed Clara. She grabbed the other and did the same.

'Um . . .' said Harry. 'This is a wee bit awkward. Um . . . I'm trying to find a woman I was dancing wi' at the ball . . . the one in the pink and gold dress. Tell ye the truth, I'm desperate to find her.'

'Why, yes, of course,' said Kara. 'I shouldn't be surprised you don't recognise me in my ordinary clothes. I look just a fright!'

'Um . . . I'm sorry, but . . . I don't think it was you,' said Harry, shrugging awkwardly.

'Are you calling my daughter a liar?' demanded her father.

[134]

'Don't listen to her!' said Clara, pushing herself in front of Kara. 'I was the one you danced with at the ball! Don't you recognise me?'

'Sorry, um . . . I don't think it was you either.'

'Are you calling at least one of my daughters a liar?' demanded their father.

Harry tensed up, and looked like he would rather be anywhere else in the world. 'Um . . .' He produced a shoe from his largest jacket pocket. *The* shoe. 'The woman . . . she, um . . . you? Um . . . she left this. I've been looking for her, and I thought if I find someone who was at the ball and fits the shoe . . . well, she's probably the wan, know what I mean?'

'Oh, you are clever,' said Kara. She snatched the shoe from him and ran upstairs with it, calling, 'Back in a moment!'

Clara followed.

Only then did Ella feel it safe to come out from the conservatory. 'Um . . . hi,' she whispered nervously. She wanted to chew her hair, but thought better of it.

Her foster father shot her a piercing glare.

'Mr Charmaine,' he said, 'I'd like you to meet Ella. A child we've been fostering. We're a –' he laughed '– a big-hearted family, you know.'

'Hi,' Harry responded absently, barely glancing at her.

'I'm no a child, I'm a woman,' Ella informed her foster father with a small smile. 'I'm the same woman you were dancing with at the ball, Harry; playing fitba' wi' the balloon.'

Harry looked up and down the young lady who stood before him, hair all over the place, faded brown polo shirt tucked into her worn, beige cords.

'Look into my eyes, Harry. Then ye'll see who I really am.'

He did. And he did. 'It's really you!'

'Aye,' said Ella, laughing with delight. 'It's really me. Now . . . was there something you wanted to say to me?'

'Aye,' said Harry. 'I love you and I want to marry you.'

'Och, is that all?' answered Ella, and threw her arms around him.

They were interrupted by a scream of pain from upstairs, followed by an agonised cry of 'Change of plan! You marry Harry and I'll do the sawing!'

'We'd better tell those two what's going on afore they amputate each other's toes,' said Ella.

'Now wait just a minute,' Ella's foster father said sternly. 'Ella's under my care. She can't get married without my permission. Of course, I'm happy to discuss the matter with a gentleman of your means. I'm sure we can work something out . . .'

'Um . . . I think that's no actually true,' murmured Harry. 'Even if someone's in care, I reckon they can marry at sixteen without permission in Scotland.'

'Ha ha!' said Ella, cheerfully.

The two ugly sisters came down. Kara was cradling the shoe and limping slightly.

'Now may I please have my shoe back?' asked Ella.

Kara backed off, startled, and clutched it tightly to her.

'Give her the shoe!' her dad snapped. She threw it at Ella.

Ella slipped her foot into the shoe. Not only was it a perfect fit, but it shimmered and sparkled with a strange yellow light . . . and then turned back into the tatty, cheap, pink trainer it was to begin with.

Kara gasped.

Clara fainted.

Their father said, 'My word!'

Harry grinned and said, 'You're some woman.'

But before any of them had fully digested what they had seen, there was a knock at the door.

Ella's foster father opened it . . . to admit her social worker. She didn't shut the front door behind her.

'Oh, hello,' she said, upon seeing Harry Charmaine. 'This is a surprise. I might ask you for your autograph for my daughter in a minute.'

'No problem,' smiled the football star.

'But first, to business,' she smiled at Ella. 'Ella, I'm glad I caught you here, because I have a surprise for you . . .' she turned around and called, 'You can come in, now.'

In walked Ella's mum.

Ella stood, stunned for a second, not quite able to believe her eyes.

'Mum?' she finally breathed.

'I got released,' said Ella's mum, while Ella sobbed into her shoulder. 'I asked the social worker to keep it a surprise. I hope you don't mind.'

'No,' said the smothered voice of Ella. 'It's a lovely surprise.'

'I'm as surprised as you are . . . I didnae know I had a parole hearing until they came for me. They seemed to think I knew all about it! Funny the things that can happen, eh?'

Ella had the first spark of suspicion in her mind about what might be going on. She whispered in her mother's ear: 'Was there a lovely, middle-aged lady in a sparkly blue dress on the parole board?'

Her mum frowned and nodded.

'Talk to ye about it later,' whispered Ella.

'Mrs McCinder,' said Harry.

'Miss McCinder.'

'Miss McCinder . . . I care aboot your daughter very much, which is why I'm here . . .'

'We'll talk about it over dinner,' said Ella's mum. 'And you can call me . . .' she hesitated. 'Actually, ye can keep calling me *Miss McCinder* until ye start knocking them in for Celtic again!'

Ella and Harry laughed.

'Anyway,' said the social worker. 'I've spoken to my superiors, and we're quite happy for you to go home today, Ella, but it will take a Children's Panel decision to officially restore custody to your mum.'

Ella burst into tears again, and sat on the floor. 'I'm going home! I'm actually going home!'

'Aye,' said her mum. 'Away and pack your things.'

'Afore I do,' said Ella, 'I have a complaint to make against this family . . .'

'Come now, Ella,' said her former foster father with a forced laugh. 'This is a happy occasion. Let's not ruin it with this sort of nonsense!'

Ella stood up and looked him straight in the eye. That was when she realised for the first time that she was taller than him. This was her moment of triumph.

'Your daughters tellt me – and you never said a word against it – that if I said anything aboot the way I was getting treated you'd make sure I would get sent somewhere even worse. Well noo I know that's no gonnae happen, I'm spilling the beans!'

And she told her social worker all the details of her mistreatment.

At one point the social worker gently restrained her mother from attacking them – holding her wrist gently, but with a subtle strength that said she could break it if she had to. 'You've only just got out of jail,' she whispered. 'Don't be sending yourself back now!'

To Ella, she said, 'You should have told me about this in the first place. I'll make sure this matter is thoroughly investigated. In the meantime, get your things. You're going home.'

'She'll be here soon,' said Dragonman. 'Don't panic.'

'Aye,' said Crabbit impatiently. She was pacing like a caged animal around the fallen Snowy. 'This is me no panicking.'

'Nononononononono,' Nono remarked sadly.

Dagger kicked Snowy. 'Get up!' he snarled. Then he shrugged. 'Just checking.'

'Who would do this to him?' asked Glaikit.

'What's he still on the flair for?' demanded Crabbit. 'We should at least make him comfy.'

'I don't think he minds much either way . . .' Dragonman was silenced by Crabbit's lopsided glare. 'Tell you what, why don't we make him comfortable?'

The Freaks all helped to lift Snowy onto the sofa and cover him with a blanket.

Then they waited impatiently for Jill to arrive.

A medium-sized eternity passed before Jill burst in the door.

She wasted no time in going straight to the sofa where Snowy lay and examining him.

'Thanatosium,' she said. 'His only hope is true love's kiss and he must get it within three days.'

'Way ahead o' ye,' said Crabbit.

'Well, if he's got a girlfriend, or a boyfriend, or whatever, or if he's in love wi' someone, we need to track them doon fast.' She was breathless now, and trying not to cry. 'It's a really slim chance.'

'No as slim as you might think, Jill,' said Crabbit. 'There is such a woman. We've already tracked her down.'

'I . . . I don't under –'

'It's you, ya dafty!'

It took a moment for Crabbit's words to sink in.

'Did he tell you that?'

'Aye.'

'Well, he must've been joking. I mean . . . I've only met him the once, and that was to bundle him into a taxi and send him here.'

'Some people don't need more,' insisted Crabbit. 'Anyways, I can assure you he was not joking!'

'It's impossible. I mean, look at me! I'm no exactly the prettiest woman in Scotland.'

Crabbit snorted. 'All normals look the same to me, so I cannae comment. But you look awright from where I'm standing. But it's no what I think and it's no what you think that coonts. It's what he thinks.'

'It's just. . . it's just so hard to believe.'

'He says he loves you, Jill,' Crabbit told her gently. 'And ye know that cannae be bad.'

'Stop blethering,' Dagger growled, waving his knives about dangerously. 'Start kissing.'

'He's right,' said Crabbit. 'Just snog the lad and see what happens. I guarantee it won't make him any worse!'

Jill nodded and knelt before Snowy. He looked just as if he were sleeping, just as beautiful as when he was healthy.

She touched his cheek. He was still warm. Apart from being clinically dead, there didn't seem to be much wrong with him.

She stroked his snowy-white hair and leant over him.

Closer and closer she drew, until finally, as softly as you like, she allowed her lips to touch his.

His eyes snapped open.

CHAPTER 15

Ella and her mum invited Harry for dinner. They laughed and chatted about football, and all three were as happy as they'd been in a long, long time.

The following Saturday, Harry knocked in a hat-trick against Rangers, prompting headlines such as: HAT-TRICK HERO HARRY: 'MY ELLA INSPIRED ME!' which, in turn, prompted Jack to grumble to his sister that she could've waited until *after* the Old Firm derby to set her Fairy Godmaw on the happy couple.

Ella received a large amount of compensation from her former foster family, which she publicly donated to charity, telling journalists: 'What dae I want wi' money? I'm marrying Harry Charmaine!'

'So tell me, mirror, and tell me true,' said King, a satisfied grin spreading across his wicked face, 'Who is *now* the bonniest *living* man in the Greater Glasgow Area?'

The mirror yawned. 'Alas, Mr King, it's still Snowy White.'

'That's impossible!' snarled King. 'I killed him myself!'

'You poisoned him with a magical poison, which is essentially a spell,' the mirror explained patiently. 'Every spell has a counter-spell, and true love's kiss is the antidote to yours. Unfortunately, your beautiful victim got it in time.'

'What?' roared King. 'Inconceivable!'

'No, Mr King, I'm telling you the truth. And you'll never guess who he got it off of? Your ex-girlfriend! How's that for an irony?'

King fumed. The mirror seemed to be enjoying his frustration.

'How did ye no just slash his throat like a normal psycho?'

King lost what remained of his temper. He picked up a chair and slung it with all his might at the mirror . . . and it bounced back with a flash of golden, magical light.

King was pulled out of his rage for a moment by bewilderment.

The horrible, twisted face in the mirror let out a demonic sigh. 'I can only be destroyed by a magical object, Mr King. As far as you're concerned I'm indestructible.'

For the first time, King was scared of his mirror, and backed away. 'You're a monster!'

'Aye,' said the mirror. 'So are you, but a monster of a different sort.'

'I'm no a monster,' said King. 'At least . . . I don't want to be.'

The mirror could tell that King was starting to doubt himself. Its favourite toy might not want to play anymore, and that could not be allowed.

'Mr King, I am your friend,' it said softly. 'Your only friend. Now, you have earned the right to get whatever you want. You have earned the right to be the bonniest man in Glasgow. That means Snowy White must die.'

'Aye,' said King.

'Good. Glad we're agreed. Now, I can help you . . . but you're gonnae have to stop trying to kill me, because frankly, it's a wee bit rude.'

'Aye, you're right,' said King. 'Snowy must die, and I need your help.'

There was just a hint of doubt creeping into his voice.

A magical object which could destroy the mirror was being tossed into the air and caught again by Crabbit as she waited outside the Adelphi Centre in the Gorbals.

She had arranged to meet Jill outside her workplace on her lunch break.

'Hi, Crabbit,' said Jill.

Crabbit caught the crystal ball and held onto it. 'Hi, Jill.'

'This is the first time you've been outside the house in years, isn't it?'

'Aye.'

'How do you feel?'

'Terrified.' Crabbit sighed, 'but the cloaking spell is gone. Oor hoose isnae safe anymore, and wi' Demenscient dead, we don't need it anymore. Me and the boys think it's time to take our chances in the real world.'

'Good for you,' said Jill.

'How's Snowy?'

'Still shaken,' said Jill. 'That's to be expected, I suppose. Being deid fair takes it oot o' ye.'

'Aye.'

'He's staying at Jack's for now. We reckon that's the safest place for him, 'cause Jack can call the sword if necessary.'

'Good plan. How are you doing? And how are you and him doing?'

Jill laughed. 'Desperate for gossip?'

'We don't get much of it when it's just the five of us, so you cannae blame me really.'

Jill shrugged and folded her arms. 'I don't know . . . it's awkward. I mean, we've no really spoken since . . . and I've never really bought into the whole *love at first sight thing*, you know? I mean, you have to get to know someone first. I dunno. We've certainly got a lot to talk aboot.'

'Aye,' said Crabbit. 'I'm sure it'll work itself out. Anyway,' she held up the ball, 'what I wanted to see you aboot was . . . I reckon this baby will not only help us locate King's mirror, but since it's a magical object, it would make a pretty large hole in it.'

'Now, that is good news,' smiled Jill.

'Thought you'd approve. So, I was thinking of taking away King's favourite toy for good. Wanna come?'

'Aye,' said Jill, 'more than anything, but I've got to be the one to do it.'

'Agreed,' said Crabbit, tossing the crystal ball into the air and catching it again. 'Boy, this is gonna be fun!'

But Fate, it seemed, was in one of its moods. For at the exact moment she went to catch the ball, she heard a car horn sound from Ballater Street. She wasn't used to hearing car horns, so she started and dropped the ball. It hit the ground, rolled along a bit, and went down a drain with a sickening *PLOP!*

'Um . . . oops?' shrugged Crabbit.

'*Oops*'?' screamed Jill. 'Crabbit, do you realise what you've done?'

'Awright, keep yer knickers on!' snapped Crabbit. She knelt down and stuck her arm in as far as it would go. 'Yeuch!' she cried. 'You know, they really should cover this thing up. Somebody could break an ankle!'

'Any joy?'

'Naw, sorry, I cannae reach it.' She withdrew her arm, which was covered in gunk, and wiped it on her clothes.

Jill groaned. 'Here, let me try,' she insisted. She got on her knees and stuffed her right arm in, but she didn't fare even so well as Crabbit. From her wrist, her arm was wider than the opening into which she was attempting to stuff it. 'Ah. Now that's embarrassing.'

'Maybe I could wrap bandages really tight around your arm . . .'

Jill glared at Crabbit and wiped her hand on her.

Their exchange was interrupted by a loud 'Ribbit!' from behind them.

They turned to see a dark green frog about the size of a fist.

'Forgive my eavesdropping,' said the frog. 'What is it thou hast lost?'

'A crystal ball,' said Jill, 'which is very, very important to us.'

'You couldnae nip doon and grab it for us, could you?' said Crabbit.

'Indeed, it would be a simple matter,' said the frog, 'but I must ask a favour.'

'Name it,' said Jill.

'Upon my return with thy crystal ball, the green one with the strangely shaped eyes must give unto me . . . a kiss.'

'Snog a frog that's after stank-diving?!' exploded Crabbit. 'Nae chance!'

'Crabbit!' pleaded Jill.

'Please thyself,' said the frog, and turned to hop away.

'Wait,' said Jill. 'I'll kiss you.'

[144]

'I regret, fair lady, that that is not an acceptable option. For my amphibian senses tell me clearly that thou art already betrothed.'

'I most certainly am not!' insisted Jill.

'In thy heart, thou art,' said the frog. 'The distinction matters not to me.'

'Crabbit, promise you'll kiss the frog!' insisted Jill. 'It's really, really, really important!'

'Yuck!' insisted Crabbit, folding her arms.

'Crabbit, please,' said Jill. 'There's them that would say a kiss fae you isnae worth raffling!'

'The fair lady must make her own decision,' the frog informed her flatly.

Crabbit chuckled. '*Fair lady?* Aye, awright then. Just because you've got a sense of humour . . . away and fetch oor ball for us. There'll be a wee kiss waiting for you when you come back.'

So the frog hopped – *PLOP!* – down the drain, and returned presently, climbing up the walls of the drain with his back legs and clinging fast to the crystal ball. He returned it to Crabbit with a solemn bow.

'Thank you,' said Crabbit.

'Thou art welcome,' said the frog. 'Now . . . to thy part in our agreement.'

Crabbit grimaced. 'Do I have to keep my promise to a frog?'

'Shame on you, Crabbit!' cried Jill, trying not to smirk. 'A promise is a promise.'

So Crabbit took the frog in one hand, and holding her long, pointed nose out the way with the other, she raised the frog to her lips to give it a kiss.

Luckily, the Adelphi Centre's car park was almost deserted, and those few who were around were facing the other way. For as soon as Crabbit's lips touched the frog's, there was a blinding flash of blue light . . . and standing before her was a seven-foot naked black man, handsome as handsome could be.

Slightly stunned and at a loss for something to say, she remained silent for several seconds, before nodding curtly. 'Awright?'

'My lady,' said the man with a bow. 'It has been many centuries since I enjoyed the benefits of human form. In my kingdom, I was a prince and first in line for the throne, but my scheming younger brother employed the services of an evil witch to bind me in the form of a frog, so that he could be King. I searched and I searched for the solution to my problem, and I finally learned that my only hope to have the spell lifted was for a lady to kiss me of her own volition, and that I must marry her for the transformation to become permanent. I also learned that though I may ask directly for a kiss, I may not explain the reason beforehand, or the spell would be useless.'

'Oh, my,' said Crabbit, suddenly becoming very girlish and giggly. 'Kissing gets a lot done in the magical world, doesn't it?'

'Aye,' said Jill.

'Um . . . could this guy borrow your jacket, Jill? He's a wee bit, um . . . exposed to the Glasgow weather.'

Jill handed him her jacket, which he had to wear around his middle.

'I am eternally in thy debt. Be my wife, that I might never have to return to the form of a frog.'

'Aye, awright, then,' said Crabbit. 'It's no like I've had any better offers.'

'Well, yous pair have a lot to talk aboot,' said Jill. 'I've got to get back to work. Meet me here aboot five, okay? We'll go do that thing wi' the mirror.'

The mirror knew they were coming and it knew why. It also knew there was nothing it could do about it, except torment them a bit first. It heard them picking the lock and creeping into the room.

'Well, if it isn't Frankenstein's Monster and Mrs Blobby. And who have they brought with them for company? A frog that the slightly uglier one turned into a man. Nicely done. Between you and me, I can't think of any other earthly way you could pull. Since marrying for love is overrated, I say congratulations.'

'Tread carefully,' said the Frog Prince. 'I am certain it is a demon!'

The mirror laughed. 'Well, *duh!* So . . . what can I do for you three ladies?'

'Die,' Jill informed it, simply.

'Long time, no see, my dear Jill-atinous blob.' The mirror cackled. 'Get it? Jill-atinous?'

Jill looked it in the eye. This pathetic creature, this mere object, had once driven her to attempt suicide. Now she was the one with the power. She finally felt no fear.

'Your words can't bring me down, mirror. Not anymore.'

'Oh, but they will. Oh, no the day. Your heid's too full of thoughts of destroying me, your lardy body too full of adrenaline and excitement. No, my taunts won't get you now, but they'll get you. They'll get you when you're walking down the street and some ned shouts something nasty. They'll get you in quiet moments when there's nothing much happening at work. They'll get you last thing at night before you go to sleep. These are the times your head will fill with my singing: "Jilly's got a ten-ton-bum, Doo-dah, Doo-dah."

'You see, you can destroy this form, this mirror, but I'm not worried, because I'll live on. I have always existed, and will always exist in the darkest corners of everybody's soul.'

'Nice speech,' said Crabbit, unimpressed. 'Ye been rehearsing that?'

The mirror had no answer.

'You know,' said Crabbit, idly tossing and catching the crystal ball, 'you could've saved us all a lot of trouble if you'd just said, "It's a matter of opinion" in the first place.'

'Aye,' said the mirror, 'but that wouldn't have been much fun, though, would it?'

'Do it, Jill!' cried Crabbit, tossing her the crystal ball.

Jill caught it and pitched it into the centre of the glass in one smooth motion.

The mirror shattered.

The piercing sound of glass shattering faded into silence.

'Thou hast done a good deed,' remarked the Frog Prince.

'Nicely done, Jill,' said Crabbit. 'How do you feel?'

[147]

'Free,' said Jill. 'Free for the first time in my life.'

Crabbit smiled. 'Gaun yersel'.'

Jill stepped forward to the remains of the mirror, pulled a tissue from her handbag, and stooped to pick up a sharp shard, which she carefully wrapped up and put it in her handbag.

'Souvenir?' asked Crabbit.

'I need to keep a bit. I'll stick it to the wall somewhere I can ayeways see it. I need it to remind me of something.'

'Gonnae share?'

'It's just that . . . believe it or not, the mirror did me a favour. See, that voice in my heid, that says all them horrible things . . . it's been there since long before I met the mirror. But noo I know where it's coming from. So I can tell it to sod off!'

King arrived home to be met with the uneasy feeling he was not alone.

'Who's there?' he demanded.

'Only us,' said Dragonman, leaping out from a cupboard.

He was joined by Nono, Glaikit and Dagger, emerging silently from their hiding places.

King was desperately afraid. He had never seen such a sight before as these . . . *creatures*: an oval-headed dwarf whose head spun wildly as he cried 'Nonononono!' in an alien voice; a man who seemed more crocodile than man; a man who seemed more gorilla than man; and what his mind could only describe as a vampire with knives for hands.

'Wha– What do you want?' stammered King. 'You want m-money? You can have it!'

'Oh, you poor, confused fellow,' said Dragonman. 'We have no interest in money. You tried to kill our brother. In fact, in a sense, you succeeded. He was effectively dead for some time. In our family, we have a code that says we don't just walk away from something like that.'

'Yeah!' snarled Dagger.

'Nonononononononono!' Nono agreed vigorously.

[148]

King backed off. 'You stay away from me, you hear? I am a very powerful man. I can have you all shot!'

'You *were* a very powerful man,' Dragonman corrected, 'thanks to your mirror. Our friends have dealt with that. Now you are nothing but a pretty face, and in just a wee minute, you'll be nothing. Hold him down, boys.'

Nono and Glaikit held King, pinning his arms and legs. King struggled, but for all his strength, he was no match for the Freaks.

Dragonman sprayed something on his face, which numbed it. 'That is so it won't hurt much,' he explained. 'We're not completely devoid of mercy. Dagger . . . ?'

In a flurry of movement lasting less than a second, Dagger drew a roadmap of scars upon King's face.

Dragonman then put circles of flame-retardant material over King's eyes, and breathed fire upon him until he was covered in blisters.

King realised that they were not trying to kill him, or even torture him physically, but he would never be the bonniest man in Glasgow again. In fact, he would never be in the top half-million. He wished that they hadn't numbed him, because then the physical agony would distract him from the mental anguish of losing the only thing he cared about.

He screamed, 'Noooooooooooooooooooooooooooooooooo!'

And Nono said, 'Yes.'

CHAPTER 16

Liz Cameron's favourite haunt was a pub in Glasgow with very expressive décor.

The cushions on the seats were blue. The cover of the pool table was blue. Nearly every square inch of wall was covered with pictures of Rangers legends, or a signed Rangers strip behind glass, or a Union Flag.

There was no need for any sign to say, 'No Football Colours': everyone knew as soon as they walked in which football colours were and weren't welcome.

The moment Rapunzel stepped in, she was the focus of many stares.

'Awright, boys!' cried Liz, stretching upwards to put a hand on Rapunzel's shoulder. 'This is my future daughter-in-law, Rapoodle!'

Rapunzel opened her mouth to correct her, then thought better of it.

Those who had been staring at Rapunzel grunted, then went back to watching the match.

'Look at that, we're late,' grumbled Liz (who was already deep into her day's drinking). She shook a fist at the giant screen, shouted 'Intae them!' then waddled up to the screen and squinted until she knew what the score was, then waddled to a barstool and climbed onto it.

Rapunzel sat down gracefully beside her.

'So you're marrying oor Jack?' the bartender asked Rapunzel.

'Yes, that's right,' she replied.

'Wouldnae have thought you were his type,' he said, conversationally. 'Still, life's full of wee surprises, eh?'

An old man with a bright red nose, who had been reading a newspaper in a corner, suddenly threw it down in disgust. 'Away back to yer ain country!' he cried, and stormed out.

'Och, don't mind him,' said Liz. 'He's a pillock, that yin.'

Rapunzel stared into her glass. 'It was very good of you to invite me out for drinks, Mrs Cameron.'

'Och, you just call me Liz, Hen,' said Liz. 'Or Maw, if ye like.'

Suddenly Rapunzel felt something she had not felt in a long time, had hoped she would never feel again.

She looked around and saw the short, hooded figure disappearing through the door.

'Excuse me,' she said to Maw and left the pub. She followed Rumpelstiltskin to a deserted alleyway.

'You came,' said Rumpelstiltskin. 'Are you not afraid?'

'If you have something to say, say it,' said Rapunzel.

'I have come a long way to find you. Or, rather . . . to find my daughter. Surrender her now and you need not die.'

'I'm not afraid of you,' said Rapunzel. 'My daughter and I are protected by the King of the Beanstalk and his magical sword! More than this, I know your name!'

Rumpelstiltskin backed off. 'You overestimate your defences. One man and one weapon do not an army make, and soon that word will lose its power over me. Then I will take what is mine, and spill the blood of any who are in my way.'

'Haw!' came a voice from behind Rapunzel.

She turned around to see Maw bearing down fast upon Rumpelstiltskin. 'That's my future daughter-in-law-to-be, gonnae be, and that,' she roared. 'You leave her alane, or I'll rip oor yer insides and feed them to ye, right?'

[151]

With that, she kicked Rumpelstiltskin so hard he would not have flown harder into the wall behind him if he were a football.

'I'll be back,' gasped the winded Rumpelstiltskin, and vanished.

It was a glorious day. The sun was beating down on Glasgow Green, and every breath of air became a smile.

Near the edge of the park was a tree so perfect for sitting in, Ella had always called it 'the Perfect Tree'. The angle of the trunk was so gentle one could almost walk up to an alcove which seemed designed for picnicking in, and could seat two comfortably.

'It was nicer afore they chopped off all the higher branches,' grumbled Ella. 'But this tree's still my favourite part of Glasgow.'

'Aye,' said Harry. 'It's nice.'

They could hear passers-by saying, 'Oh, look! That's Harry Charming!' and, 'Och, leave him alane, he's up a tree wi' his bird.'

They sat in silence awhile, stroking each other's fingers.

'So . . . what kinda music are ye into or that?' said Harry.

'Mozart,' said Ella, blushing slightly. 'I know, I know. I'm seventeen years old and I'm no a toff, so what am I doing into classical music?'

'Ye can like what ye like,' shrugged Harry. 'Doesnae matter.'

'It's just . . . he takes me places in my mind nae other music does, you know? Places where it's okay to be me. Does that make any sense?'

'Aye,' said Harry, smiling. 'Aye, it does. I'm into Rage Against the Machine and a' that.'

'It's great how we're that different, isn't it?' said Ella.

'Aye.'

Ella breathed the warm, fresh air, and felt totally relaxed and happy. 'I love it here,' she said. 'We should get married here!'

'What?'

'Outdoor wedding, here in Glasgow Green! That would be so perfect!'

'Aye, but . . . ye cannae trust the weather in Glasgow to stay like this, can ye?'

'We'll get a giant marquee or something! Come on, it'll be beautiful.'

Harry smiled. He looked around him at the green grass, the trees, the children playing, the Clyde in the background and the People's Palace in the distance.

He couldn't think of a single reason to disagree.

There was no small amount of awkwardness between Snowy and Jill as they sat eating sandwiches on a bench in Buchanan Street.

Snowy had a distant, haunted look about him that worried Jill.

'What are you thinking?' she asked.

'About being dead,' he answered honestly. 'About how some day we'll all be dead and there's nothing we can do about it. About how I've *been* dead, but I still couldn't tell you what it's like. About how it would never have happened if I wasn't so *stupid*.'

'You're no stupid, Snowy.'

'I accepted sweets from a stranger when I *knew* there was someone out there trying to kill me,' said Snowy. 'I'd say that qualifies as stupid.'

Jill shrugged. 'Well, when you put it that way . . . But everyone's stupid sometimes. Look at me: I've got six Highers, and I'd still be a' day shoving my weight into a door that says, "Pull". She put a hand on his shoulder. 'Nae sense beating yerself up aboot it. You're alright noo. You're definitely not stupid.'

Snowy smiled at her. She was such a warm person. That had been obvious the first time he had looked into those big, brown eyes.

'Tell you what,' he said, 'I'll admit I'm not stupid, if you'll admit you're beautiful.'

Jill smiled and blushed. 'It's no that easy.'

'Why not?'

'Because I've . . . I've reconciled myself to being a big, fat lump. I'm okay with it, now.'

'Fat is relative,' shrugged Snowy. 'If my mother were to see you, she'd say, "That lass doesn't eat enough," and start shovelling haggis down you as a matter of urgency.'

[153]

Jill laughed out loud. 'No likely. I'm a vegetarian.'

'If you told her that, she'd faint.' Snowy stroked her hair. 'You have great beauty, Jill. It's not the sort of beauty that gets you on the cover of a magazine, but that's not the sort of beauty a man remembers for long. Your beauty has nothing to do with how fat or thin you are. It comes from deep inside you and shines through your eyes and your smile. It's the sort of beauty that can get right into a man's soul and make him love you at a glance . . . which is the only reason I'm here, after all.'

Jill avoided his gaze. On the one hand, she enjoyed the flattery. On the other, she was unused to it, and had absolutely no idea how to deal with it.

'Come on,' she said. 'I said I'd show you the sights.'

'Wheeeeeeeeeeeeeeeeeeeeeeeeeeeeeeeeeeeeeeeeeeeeeeeeee!'

A doorway in Buchanan Street, which appeared at a glance to lead to just another shop, actually led into Princes Square, which Jill described as 'the prettiest mall in Glasgow'.

She never could resist going up the escalators at the near end, crossing over to the far end, and sliding down the banister there. This time she was doing so with Snowy on her knee.

They were both helpless with laughter when they landed at the feet of a stern security guard.

'I thought I tellt you no to come back in here!' he growled at Jill, then escorted them from the premises.

'Well,' said Jill, 'was that worth getting flung oot for?'

'Absolutely!' cried Snowy.

They walked past a shut-down bookshop, now dark and empty. Jill's smile faded.

'Heart and soul got ripped right oot Buchanan Street when that closed,' she mused sadly. 'It'll never be the same again.'

Snowy squeezed her hand sympathetically.

'See them lights?' said Jill. Several rows of lights were strung between the bookshop and the adjacent building. 'Used to be ye could go up the stairs by the window in the bookshop, and you'd reach a point where the lights outside were at your feet.

'I always thought it looked just like a sparkly floor. Like you could just walk across it to the office over there, chap their windae and run away!'

Snowy smiled.

Jill sighed. 'I miss that shop.'

They walked up Buchanan Street, where everyone was marching unconsciously to the rhythm of their nearest busker: a saxophonist in the alleyway to the Gallery of Modern Art; a bit further up, two reggae singers with electric guitars; further still, a lone piper.

'Sometimes I walk up and doon Buchanan Street just because I love it,' Jill explained. 'It's so alive, you know. Ye can really dance to the heartbeat of Glasgow here. Feel it coming up through the soles o' yer shoes.'

'Aye,' said Snowy.

They reached the top of Buchanan Street, where Donald Dewar's statue stood looking over the city, his glasses permanently stolen.

'This is my favourite spot,' said Jill. She looked down the street on a hill, whose tunnel-like structure showed only a slice of a view at the bottom, which went on for miles and miles, through the South Side of Glasgow, all the way to the hills beyond. It was breathtakingly beautiful.

A cold wind blew her hair all over the place.

'Unfortunately, it is a bit of a wind-tunnel . . .'

'Aye,' said Snowy. 'You'll soon ken if your fly's undone in that!' He took her by the hand and said, 'Thank you for showing me Glasgow. Your Glasgow, I mean.'

Jill grinned. 'My Glasgow. I like that. It's true, I suppose. Everyone's got their ain personal Glasgow.'

'Mine is wonderful, because you're in it.'

Her eyes lit up. 'I feel beautiful when I'm with you.'

'Well . . . I suppose I'll just have to stay with you, then.'

Then they kissed.

CHAPTER 17

'KING DISFIGURED BY THUGS!' cried a headline, as King insisted in an interview that he was famous because of his talent, not his looks; that *of course* he would keep doing *The Reggie King Show*; that he was still the same person and nothing had really changed.

Later that week, *The Reggie King Show* was cancelled.

King sat alone in his home, for the first time in years not feeling up to working out. He had no job, no mirror and had lost his looks.

He still wanted White dead, of course, but now it was from sheer spite.

As for the . . . the *monsters* who had done this to him . . . Yes, he would like to see the end of them, too. But without his mirror, it seemed impossible.

He was distracted from his thoughts by an unexpected sound.

The sound of breathing.

'Who's there? Show yourself!' he demanded, terrified.

'A friend,' came the voice, and from the shadows strutted the Wolf.

'What are you doing in my house?'

'Relax,' said the Wolf. 'I'm on your side. You were a customer of mine, once, don't you remember? Though it's true, we never met face-to-face. I'm the Big, Bad Wolf.' He extended a paw.

King simply stared at it.

'Mr King, I have a proposition for you.' The Wolf pointed to his own injuries. 'This was done to me by three little pigs.'

'What's that to me?' demanded King.

'I had hoped you would feel some sort of kinship,' said the Wolf, 'since you and I were both scarred for life by our enemies. I, for one, want vengeance. Don't you?'

'What, exactly, is your proposition?' asked King.

'It's very simple, my friend. I will help you with your revenge, and you will help me with mine.'

'How?'

'My sources tell me that you have quite an interesting mirror.'

King covered up his fear by pretending to laugh. His mind was racing. The Wolf obviously didn't know the mirror had been destroyed or he wouldn't be here. King knew any chance of an alliance relied upon the Wolf's remaining in the dark.

'Your sources are good,' said King. 'That item is a fairly well-kept secret.'

'No one keeps a secret from the Big, Bad Wolf for very long, Mr King.' The Wolf grinned hungrily. 'I think you have most likely guessed the details of my proposition. You will ask your mirror to tell you where the three little pigs are hiding, then report back to me. I, in return, will dispose of those whose existence is so troublesome to you.'

King nodded. 'It sounds like a good deal, but I would like you to deliver your part of the bargain first.'

'Why, Mr King, don't you trust me? I must say, I'm hurt.'

King shrugged, smiling as pleasantly as he could. 'You're a vicious, amoral wolf who's broken into my home. If I was you and you was me, would you trust you?'

The Wolf laughed. 'A gentleman's word has always been good enough for me, Mr King, for the simple reason that if it isn't, I rip his throat out. For this reason alone, I agree to your terms.'

'Then we have an accord,' said King, and he shook the Wolf's paw. 'Now get out of my house.'

It was a curious thing, but even after the Wolf had left, King could not shake the feeling that he was not alone in the room.

'Who's there?' he demanded.

'A friend,' hissed an evil voice.

'Don't any of my friends knock?' demanded King. 'Show yourself!'

A small, hooded figure with red, glowing eyes appeared before him.

'I'm calling the police,' insisted King.

'By all means,' replied Rumpelstiltskin, appearing and disappearing several times just to demonstrate that he could. 'You will succeed in convincing them that you are crazy, and that would amuse me.'

'Who ... *what* are you?'

'My name does not concern you,' said Rumpelstiltskin. 'I have come to help you, and to offer you a gift.'

'I don't accept gifts from strangers,' said King. 'It's a bad idea!'

'You will accept this one if you are not a fool.' Rumpelstiltskin held his tiny, gnarled hands high and yelled, 'Club!'

A wooden club, twice the length of the elf's body, appeared in his hands. 'For you.'

King picked up the club and examined it. 'Why would I want this? It's a hunk of wood.'

Rumpelstiltskin picked up the hunk of wood and brought it down upon the coffee table. There was a crackle, and what looked like lightning and the table shattered into tiny splinters of wood.

'I barely tapped it,' said Rumpelstiltskin. 'I overheard your conversation with the Big, Bad Wolf. My sources are ahead of his, it would seem: I know that your mirror is no more.'

'So?'

'So, you play a dangerous game, Mr King. When the Wolf learns he has been cheated, he will be disappointed in you, and those who disappoint the Wolf do not have a high life expectancy. I can protect you from his wrath.'

King stood up solemnly and looked at his charred and scarred face in the mirror on the wall. 'Everything I ever gave a hoot aboot is gone. See after Snowy and the Freaks are deid and buried? I don't care what happens to me. I have nothing left to live for.'

'I had thought you were stronger than that,' hissed Rumpelstiltskin. 'No matter. If you want to commit suicide after the Wolf has done your bidding, that neither concerns me nor concerns me. But if the Wolf's success is so important to you – the *only* thing that is important to you – well, if I were you, I would want some insurance. After all, how can you be sure he will succeed? How can you be certain he won't learn of your deception prematurely?'

King thought hard about that. Where was the harm in a little insurance?

'What will this ... insurance ... cost me?'

King couldn't see the creature's grin, but the sudden brightening of its eyes told him it was there.

'Jack Cameron, whom I believe you know, and his wife-to-be, the one he calls Rapunzel ... they have something which belongs to me. If you slay them both, I can take it back.'

King nodded. 'You have the magic club. How can ye no dae yer ain dirty work?'

'I'm sure you understand my reluctance to explain everything. It is enough to say ... they have a weapon. It is effective against me, but it won't harm you.'

King picked up the club and tried it himself. He knocked a large hole in the wall with a single blow.

'Okay,' said King. 'I'll take care of Jack and Rapunzel, then use the same club to get rid of Snowy and the Freaks ... with your help, I trust.'

'Absolutely.'

'And you'll keep the Wolf off my back when he realises I've been at it?'

'Absolutely.'

A grin spread across King's disfigured face, as he swung the club through the air. 'Pleasure doing business with you.'

Ella and Harry were the first to arrive at Jack's housewarming party.

'Hey, Jack,' she said, hugging him and handing him a bottle of wine.

'Come on in,' said Jack, smiling warmly.

'Ella!' cried Upenda, the instant she saw her and wasted no time in jumping into her arms.

'Hi, Upenda,' said Ella, hugging her tightly. 'It's really good to see you again!'

'It's an honour to meet you, Mr Charmaine,' said Jack, shaking the footballer's hand.

'Likewise,' said Harry. 'Call me Harry.'

Ella nearly jumped out of her skin when the ostrich nuzzled her.

'Bwarrkh!' said the ostrich.

'She likes you,' said Jack. 'Her name's Baxter, the ostrich that lays the golden eggs.'

'Hey, Baxter,' said Ella, stroking him. 'I wouldnae have called her Baxter, though,' she commented. 'She looks more like a . . . Henrik, or a Jinky. Or maybe even a Harry!'

'I felt I owed it to her to name her after a Rangers legend,' said Jack. 'You can tell by the look in her eyes she's a blue-nose.'

'I'll set the SSPCA on you,' teased Ella. 'Turning an innocent creature into a hun!'

Jack laughed.

'Oh,' said Ella. 'Nearly forgot, I brought a wee house-within-housewarming prezzie for Thumbelina.'

'Now that's what I like to hear,' cried Thumbelina, coming out of her doll's house.

'I've been dying to meet you,' said Ella, presenting her with a tiny pair of sparkly shoes.

Thumbelina tried them on. They were a perfect fit.

'Aw, you shouldnae have! Och, who am I trying to kid! Of course you should've! You can call me Thumbsy, by the way. You're my friend.' Then she added, as an afterthought, 'I'm destined to marry the King o' the Pixies!'

'Really? Congrats!'

Ella and Harry sat down on a sofa near the table, which was chock-a-block with food and drink.

'Help yersel' to whatever ye like. Treat this like yer ain hoose, you know? There's plenty there. Nearest toilet is straight across the hallway oot that door.'

'Oooh, "Nearest toilet",' mocked Ella. 'I knew him when he was dole scum,' she informed Harry in a stage whisper.

Next to arrive were the Freaks and the Frog Prince.

Introductions were made, pleasantries exchanged. Thumbelina said, 'You're right enough: they're seriously ugly!' and they all tucked into the food and drink, exchanging anecdotes and laughs.

When Jill and Snowy arrived, laughter was replaced by an awkward silence. Jill's glare at Crabbit seemed to say, *How could you?* Crabbit met her gaze unflinchingly. She was proud of what the Freaks had done.

'It's really good to meet you, Snowy,' said Ella, trying to break it up a bit. 'I almost killed you once. Hope there's nae hard feelings aboot that.'

Snowy smiled. 'I've never been one to hold a grudge.'

'Well, if that doesn't call for a hug, I don't know what does,' said Jack.

Ella and Snowy laughed, stood up and hugged each other. They got a round of applause.

The guests mostly relaxed after that, although Jill maintained a steady glare at the Freaks, of whom Crabbit was the only one who would meet her gaze.

'Look,' Crabbit said, eventually. 'We did what we had to, alright? He killed one of oor family. Aye, we were lucky enough to get him back, but he still killed him.'

'I didn't ask you to,' said Snowy.

'We have a code,' insisted Crabbit.

'And what of mercy?' said the Frog Prince.

'What?'

'Mercy,' said the Frog Prince. 'It is the quality of acting with compassion, towards thine enemies as much as thy friends.'

'I know what "mercy" means, smarty pants,' snapped Crabbit, 'and I've got to tell you, I love you, Honey, but you've got a lot to learn aboot being a Freak.'

'But I am not a Freak, I am a former frog,' the Frog Prince told her calmly. 'I have been both a frog and a man, and I have found mercy to be the very best quality of both.'

'Besides which,' Jill interjected, 'you've put all of us in danger; more danger than we were afore. You had no right.'

'Snowy's no in any more danger,' shrugged Crabbit. 'The Freaks are, but we all knew that when we made the decision to rearrange his face. I don't see how the rest of yous are in danger. In fact, he might even lay off of Snowy. Let's face it, if he wants to be the bonniest man in Glesga noo, it's an A-bomb he's wanting!'

'Anyway,' said Jill, seeing the need for a change of subject. 'Ella . . . you said you had something you wanted to talk to me aboot?'

'Yes, um . . .' Ella blushed and wriggled awkwardly. 'Actually, it's something I wanted to run by all of yous. It's probably daft . . .'

'Well, what?' said Jill, smiling. 'What is it, Ella?'

'Well,' said Ella, 'we've all become, like, really good friends . . . sort of. And we'd all be going to each other's weddings and that, so why not all get married at the same time? One big wedding, instead of four?'

'Five,' Thumbelina corrected her, grumpily.

'Look, your wedding's your ain special day, and if any of yous think it's a daft idea, we'll say no more. But I just think . . . me and Harry, you and Snowy, Crabbit and the Frog Prince and Jack and Punzy . . . and, of course, Thumbsy and the King of the Pixies, if that's on in time . . . getting married at the same time in Glasgow Green . . . I just think it would be, well, nice.' She shrugged and shifted awkwardly. 'Och, it's a daft idea.'

'Well, I think it's a dandy idea!' said Crabbit. 'Wan for a' and a' for wan and that! What do you reckon, Honey?'

'I would make thee happy,' said the Frog Prince. 'What thou wishest, so shall I do.'

Crabbit giggled like a little girl. 'Isn't he great?'

Rapunzel and Jack exchanged a glance.

'We're in,' said Rapunzel.

'What do you reckon?' Jill asked Snowy.

'I dunno. What do you reckon?'

'I dunno. What do you reckon?'

This went on for a few rounds before they dissolved in giggles, and Jill said, 'I think we're in.'

Ella grinned. 'It's gonnae be beautiful!'

Just then, the doorbell chimed. Jack got up to let in the Fairy Godmaw.

As soon as she entered the living room, Ella glomped her.

'Thank you!' cried Ella! 'Thank you so much! For everything!'

Her Fairy Godmaw laughed and kissed her forehead. 'Always a pleasure, Ella.' She freed herself from the embrace and handed a package to Jack.

'Housewarming prezzie,' she said.

The gift was large and circular, and quite heavy.

'Thanks,' Jack said, and tore the wrapping paper off.

It was a highly polished, highly decorated shield.

'That will protect you against one blow fae a magical weapon. Just the wan, mind, then its power is gone.'

'Uh-oh,' said Jack, a queasy feeling rising inside of him. 'I have the horrible feeling you're about to tell me I'm gonnae need this.'

'I wish I could tell you you're wrang,' said the Fairy Godmaw.

Jack swallowed hard.

The queasy feeling in his stomach was now in every stomach in the room.

'What's going on?' said Crabbit.

'See Reggie King? He still wants Snowy deid. And noo he's after the Freaks and all.'

'Yes, we know that,' said Jack.

'Aye, but what you don't know is that he's got help,' said the Fairy

Godmaw. 'Help fae a big, bad wolf called the Big, Bad Wolf, and also . . .
fae Rumpelstiltskin.'

Silence fell like a bomb upon the room. Everyone traded ominous glances.

Rapunzel felt her blood run cold. 'What does . . . *he* . . . have to gain by
an alliance with King?'

'He finds it hard to attack us because we know his name,' said Jack. 'The
power of that won't last forever, but it'll do for now. So he gets King to do
his dirty work, to kill us, take Upenda . . . and in exchange, he gives King
a magical weapon of some sort to finish off Snowy and the Freaks. Am I
right?'

'Aye, I'm afraid so,' sighed the Fairy Godmaw. 'It's an enchanted club.
Mair than a match for your sword, I'm afraid.'

Jack held up the shield. 'This the best ye can dae?'

'Aye. I'm forbidden to interfere in mortal affairs. Now, as you know, I've
been treating that more as a guideline than a rule, but direct intervention
in a mortal conflict . . . oot the question. Giving you that shield is probably mair than my wings are worth.'

Jack looked helplessly from the Fairy Godmaw, to Rapunzel and Upenda,
to Snowy, to the Freaks. 'I cannae protect all of yous all the time!'

'Reginald King isnae a very patient man,' said the Fairy Godmaw.
'Withoot his mirror, he'll have a hard time finding yous all. Not beyond
him, but difficult. I'll wager he's gonnae attack when he knows yous are
all gonnae be in the same place at the same time.'

Another silence, as the significance of that dawned on everyone.

Jill's eyes went wide. 'The wedding.'

No one said anything for a long moment. Finally Jill said, 'We have to
call it off.'

'Why?' cried Ella.

'What do you mean, "why?" 'Cause King's gonnae show up and kill us
all at my wedding, that's why!'

'I agree with Jill,' said Rapunzel. 'I will not put my daughter in danger.'

'Mum!' cried Upenda. 'Don't I get a say in this?'

'No, you don't.'

'Look,' said Ella. 'We're gonnae have to face him sooner or later anyway. So our options are: A: we can invite each other to our weddings, and gie him four chances instead o' wan; B: we can no invite each other to our weddings, which would suck, and he would catch up with yous eventually and pick yous off wan-by-wan; C: we could cancel all four weddings awthegether, which would suck more, and same problem. Plus you'd have to spend your whole lives in hiding. Or, D: we can stick with the plan and say, "Bring it on!" I mean, Jack said it himself: he cannae protect all of us all the time. This is oor best chance.'

'I'm wi' Ella,' said Jack. 'Nae choice.'

Dragonman cleared his throat, sending plumes of smoke into the room. 'Please correct me if I'm wrong, but I believe I speak for all the Freaks when I say . . . we will never hide again.'

The other Freaks, including Nono, nodded solemnly.

'I just want us to be clear on this,' said Jill. 'We're no just organising a wedding, we're organising a war?'

'The war's on no matter what we do, Jill,' Ella told her gently. 'And if we lose, there isnae gonnae be a wedding.'

'Let King crash the wedding,' said Jack, holding his shield aloft. 'If he does, he's getting it!'

'Jack, I need to talk to you a second,' said Jill.

Alone in the kitchen, trying to gather her thoughts and control her feelings, Jill was joined by Jack.

She had her back to him when he entered, and she didn't turn to face him.

'Are you awright?' asked Jack.

Jill folded her arms and began trembling all over. 'No, Jack, I'm no awright.' Her voice was cracking. 'I'm very, very no awright.'

Jack went to touch her, but she resisted.

'You seem,' she began, but was choked by emotion. 'You seem pretty gung-ho aboot this whole thing. I think you enjoy the role of action hero a wee bit too much for yer ain good.'

'Jill, that's not fair. I wasnae meaning to be an action hero. It just sort of . . . happened. Look at me, Jill.'

Jill turned to face him. She was crying.

'Jill, I have to be strong, or at least kid on to be strong. For my family. For you. I'm sorry if that upsets you.'

'It would be . . . it would be terrible for me to think that you were relishing the idea of killing Reggie.'

Jack's features hardened. 'You're right. It would be terrible for you to think that.'

'But you don't seem to have a lot against the idea.'

The hardness in Jack's face suddenly cracked open.

'Oh, Jill, when you get it wrong, you really . . .' He steadied himself and chewed his lips, fighting the tears. 'Jill, when I killed that giant, I . . . I don't know how to say it. I . . . I can never get back what I lost in that moment. Never. I don't like being a killer, and I certainly don't want to do it again. I cannae talk to anyone about how much it gnaws at me that I might have to!'

'Reggie was very cruel to me when I was wi' him,' Jill said, distantly, in almost a ghost of her usual voice. 'Noo he's trying to kill the man I love and a fair few of my friends . . . and you. But for a' that . . . he meant something to me once and I really don't want him to die!'

'Okay,' he said. 'It's okay. Jill, I give you my word. If I can find any way to keep everyone I love safe without killing King, I'll do it.'

The mood was sombre when Jack and Jill returned to what had started as a party.

'Okay,' said Ella. 'Decision time. If you want the joint wedding and all that comes wi' it, give me yer hand. If I don't see seven other hands, we forget the whole thing, nae questions asked.'

She reached across the table. Harry did the same and put his hand on hers.

Then Crabbit's gnarled green and the Frog Prince's giant black hand joined them. Then Rapunzel and Jack did the same. Finally, so did Jill and Snowy.

Like an eight-spoked bike wheel, they stood round the table, hand upon hand, dreading what was to come.

CHAPTER 18

'That's absolutely amazing,' said Jill.

The brides were trying on their wedding dresses in Jill's living room.

Ella beamed, twirling in her dress. 'Fairy Godmaw made me it.'

'Zip me up?' said Jill. Ella helped her with the zip at the back of her wedding dress.

'I look stupid!' insisted Crabbit, shuffling awkwardly in her wedding dress. 'Freaks like me shouldnae wear dresses like this! I mean, look at me!'

'You would rather marry in rags?' asked Rapunzel, struggling into her own dress.

'Frankly, yes. Then at least I wouldnae be a walking, talking oxymoron!'

'You look like an angel, Mum,' said Upenda.

Jill looked in the mirror and grinned. 'Look at me. I'm almost pretty.'

Ella rolled her eyes. 'Jill, you *are* pretty. You've always been pretty.' She rubbed Jill's shoulder affectionately. 'You put too much of your self-esteem in how you look, and too much of your opinion of how you look in your weight. You're the best human being I've ever met, and you're also drop-dead gorgeous. If you don't believe me, think of it this way: you've pulled the bonniest man in Glasgow. Twice!'

Jill laughed.

They heard a key turning in the lock. Ella stood back. 'Who's that?'

Jill frowned, confused. 'Cannae be Jack. He knows we're trying on dresses.'

Rapunzel ushered Upenda behind her and adopted a fighting stance. But it was Jack.

He came into the room with his head down and sank into his usual beanbag.

'Jack, get oot o' here!' cried Jill. 'Ye cannae see Punzy's dress afore the wedding!'

Jack didn't look her in the eye. They held their breath waiting for him to speak.

'Went back to Maw's to get some things,' croaked Jack. He cleared his throat to try and get control of his voice. 'She was on the floor. Massive heart attack. I phoned an ambulance and did CPR, but ... they couldnae resuscitate her. She's away.'

It was a long, yet short, and very strange day.

Everyone had gone to Jack's house after digesting the news. Phone calls were made, condolences expressed, and by the evening only Jack, Rapunzel, Upenda, Snowy, Jill and Thumbelina remained.

Jack was making coffees, and going over and over in his mind what happened; what he imagined he could have done better.

Thirty chest compressions to two breaths. He was sure that was right. But they did keep changing it.

'How are you feeling?' said Jill.

'Pretty crappy,' said Jack.

'Yeah, same here.'

'I don't know if I can do this,' said Jack.

'Do what?' said Jill.

'Anything,' said Jack. 'The wedding. Fighting King. Anything. It's easy to be brave when you've got a mammy who'd rip anyone's liver oot if they laid a finger on you, you know? And noo? Noo I just cannae dae anything. I'm sorry, it's just ... everybody's expecting me to be able to be this big, sword-waving hero ... and I'm no. No anymair.'

Jill nodded slowly. His words scared her more than anything else in the world, but she accepted them. 'Okay. Well, I don't really know what we're gonnae dae without you, but we'll talk aboot it after the funeral.'

Jack slapped his forehead. 'The funeral! God!'

'What is it?' asked Rapunzel.

Jack was biting his lip and squeezing his eyes shut. 'You cannae come. Neither can Upenda. Neither can Snowy.'

It was a thought that hadn't occurred to Jill before and it hit her like a ton of bricks. All at once she knew Jack was right. 'Security,' she grumbled.

'Aye. We think King's gonnae attack the wedding because he knows we'll all be there. So we cannae have us all at the funeral, because that could turn into a *really* crappy day!'

'I should've done more,' said Jack, still unable to believe what had happened. 'I . . . I should've been there earlier, I should've . . . I should've done something better, I should've . . . I should've saved her.'

'There was nothing you could've done,' insisted Thumbelina. 'Look, face it . . . she was sort of asking for it.'

Jill bristled. 'As always, Thumbelina, you've shown the sensitivity of a sandpaper wet wipe.'

'I'm no meaning to,' said Thumbelina. 'I'm just saying . . . she was a heart-attack waiting to happen. She smoked like a chimney, drank like a fish, and thought deep-fried pies were a light snack. Only person who could've stopped this fae happening was her ain self. If she was here she'd be the first to agree wi' me. And she'd gie you a big kick up the bum if she could hear you beat yersel' up for something you could never in a million years have done anything aboot!'

Jack balled his hands into fists. He had to be angry at *someone*. 'And you!' he suddenly snapped at Jill. 'How'd you no use magic to bring her back?'

'You know as well as I do magic doesnae work like that,' Jill replied, shaking her head sadly.

'How no?' demanded Jack, furiously.

It was Rapunzel who put her hand on him and replied, 'She's right, Jack. Magic must work always with nature, never against it.'

'No much natural aboot what I've seen o' magic,' snorted Jack.

'On the contrary,' said Rapunzel. 'Do you see nothing magical about life? About the universe? About time and space and everything that exists? Magic and nature are not two things, they are one. Just as God and nature are not two things, they are one. Just as God and love and creativity are one.

'The life of every living thing is a miracle, and nature gives it freely. But we can only have it a short time, before we move on. And that is why magic cannot bring someone back from death, and it is good that it cannot, because that's what keeps the river of life flowing.'

'Aye,' said Jill. 'What she said.'

The post-funeral wake began as a fairly boring affair, with the buzz of boring old people talking about boring old things.

When the shrivelled lady with the sandwiches arrived at Jack and Jill's table, Jill asked, 'Excuse me, do you know if there's any vegetarian sandwiches?'

The shrivelled lady looked at Jill as if she were an alien, and finally answered, 'There's tuna, Hen.'

Jill smiled a strained smile until she was out of earshot, then said, 'Sod it. I'm going for chips.'

'Thought you were trying to cut doon on chips?' said Jack.

'Naebody's perfect, Jack. You want anything?'

'Naw, I'm alright, thanks.'

'You be alright here yersel'?'

'Aye,' said Jack. 'Nae bother.'

As soon as Jill left, though, Jack found himself wanting for company. He had Thumbelina in his pocket, though, who would whisper the occasional 'You alright?' or a rude comment about Jack's elderly relatives.

Said elderly relatives seemed to be taking it in turns to come up, say, 'Och, hello! I've no seen ye in years,' and, 'That was a really good eulogy. That was oor Liz, spot on,' and, 'I hear you're getting married? I'd've thought she'd be here.'

Jack politely thanked them and told them Rapunzel was ill, but he didn't recognise any of them.

Suddenly, Jack knew he had to excuse himself. He felt something quite horrid, a sensation like something evil was around him and inside him all at once.

From the corner of his eye, he saw a dark, hooded creature with glowing red eyes, staring at him from the fire exit, and then it was gone without anyone else noticing. Although he'd never met the creature, Jack knew exactly who and what he was dealing with. He followed Rumpelstiltskin outside and into a secluded alleyway.

He grabbed the elf and pinned him against a wall. Rumpelstiltskin didn't struggle.

'Have you nae shame at all, Rumpelstiltskin?' He felt the creature weaken in his hands, heard it groan in pain. It was very satisfying. 'I've just lost my mother. You leave me and my family alane!'

'Knowing my name will not protect you forever,' said Rumpelstiltskin. 'Its power diminishes each time you use it. Soon you will be helpless.'

'I'll no be helpless if I snap your neck!'

'Do not threaten me. I come in peace, to pay my respects, and make you a proposition.'

'Don't tell me, let me guess,' said Jack. 'I have to hand my step-daughter over to you and you won't kill me or anyone I care aboot. Then you'll stop King from killing Snowy and the Freaks.' He shook his head sadly. 'So predictable. Go away, Shorty. I'm no interested.'

'Then a lot of people, including you, will die for your arrogance,' said Rumpelstiltskin. 'And the child will still be mine. Think about it.'

Jack threw him to the ground. 'Here's my counter-proposition,' he growled. 'You come near my family again . . . and I'll kill you.'

He went back inside, leaving the elf struggling to his feet.

Rumpelstiltskin was just gathering the strength to vanish, when he heard a voice behind him.

'Rumpelstiltskin?'

He knew it was not the voice of a mortal, for he felt nothing when she used that name. He turned around to face the Fairy Godmaw.

'You?' he spat.

She smiled politely. 'Before ye disappear, do you think I could have a wee word?'

Jill ate half a bag of chips, binned the rest, and took a deep breath before returning. She had hoped to get some tears out the way while no one was watching, but none would come.

She felt she had to stay impossibly strong for Jack. Oh, Jack was strong in his own way, when it came to rescuing damsels and slaying giants . . . but for coping with death, he had to lean on Jill.

When she rejoined Jack, he told her about the encounter with Rumpelstiltskin outside.

She drew a deep breath. 'We didnae need that. You awright?'

'I'm fine,' said Jack. 'But you mind what I said aboot no being able to cope?'

'Aye?'

'Well, forget it! If that midget shows up at my wedding, he's pure getting it! Same goes for King and the Wolf. They'll no be pushing me around.'

'Gaun yersel'!' came a voice from Jack's pocket.

Jill smiled. 'Nice to have the old Jack back.'

Suddenly, there was a great stir. People were shoving their chairs this way and that, to get out the way or to get a better look, and the hall echoed with cries of 'Oh, my God!' and 'What is that?' and 'Somebody step on it!'

What looked at a glance like a large bug seemed, on closer inspection, to be a very small man, with wings . . . and a lopsided crown.

He was flying, sort of, but it looked more like jumping, for he was flying drunkenly, getting a few feet into the air before crashing into something or someone.

When he reached Jack's table, he tried to fly up, crumpled his nose, and decided perhaps he'd better climb.

On reaching the top of the table, he staggered about, barely able to stand.

'Thumbelininina,' he slurred at the top of his tiny lungs. 'It is I, (hic!) the Ping of the Kixies ... I mean the King of the Pixies (hic!) yer one true love! Yer destiny! So come oot here and gie's a kiss!'

Thumbelina hopped out of Jack's pocket and down his tie.

All eyes were upon their table, and there was silence. There was no hiding the fact that Jack had had a tiny woman in his pocket all this time, or that a tiny drunk man had come to court her.

A voice whispered, 'It's witchcraft!'

'How dare you?' Thumbelina demanded. 'Two o' my best friends have just lost their mammy, and you're barging in here right after the funeral? How dare you?'

The King of the Pixies staggered a step back. 'But-but ... you and me are destined to be together! You've to be my Queen! It's destiny, so it is!'

'On yer bike, ya drunken bampot!' cried Thumbelina. 'I don't take orders fae destiny!' With that, she shoved him off the table.

'You're making a mistake!' cried the King. 'Nobody spurns the King o' the Pixies!'

He half-staggered, half-flew from the building.

'Are you sure aboot this?' Jill asked Thumbelina, gently. 'I mean, it's what you wanted. What you've dreamed aboot. What you'll no shut up aboot ...'

'Och, I don't need the likes o' him!' cried Thumbelina. 'See yous lot? Yous lot are sad, needing to be paired off afore ye can be happy! I'm happy just the way I am. Just me and my friends. I mean ... I've got amazing friends. I really do.'

Jill stroked her with a pinkie. 'You're awright, Thumbsy. You're awright.'

CHAPTER 19

The big day came, and what a lovely day it was!

Jack, Snowy, Harry and the Frog Prince stood in their kilts on Glasgow Green, awaiting their brides.

'Let's go through this one more time,' said Harry. 'I'm your Best Man ... you're Snowy's Best Man ... Snowy's the Frog Prince's Best Man ... and the Frog Prince is my Best Man.'

'Aye,' said Jack. 'It's no that hard.'

'Och, well I was only asking!' insisted Harry.

'Sorry,' said Jack. 'I didnae mean to snap.'

'That's okay,' said Harry. 'Ye nervous?'

'Aye.'

'What ye mair nervous aboot? The wedding or the war?'

Jack shook his head and tried to laugh. 'Six o' wan, half a dozen o' the other, mate.'

'So whose ring have I got?'

'Mine,' said Jack, 'because you're my Best Man.'

'So we'll be handing the rings round in a circle?'

At that, Snowy burst out laughing. 'Rings in a circle! Sorry ... I'm easily amused.'

Thumbelina popped her head out of Jack's shirt pocket. 'Never mind nervous,' she said, ominously. 'Question is, are you ready?'

'Aye,' said Jack. 'I'm ready.'

*   *   *

Jill, Ella, Crabbit and Rapunzel gathered in Jill's living room, wearing their wedding dresses, waiting for the taxi.

The atmosphere was one of dread and tension, not excitement and butterflies.

'Well,' said Ella, dryly. 'Here it is. The happiest day of our lives.'

'Aye,' said Jill.

'There will be many press photographers,' said Rapunzel. 'I am sure we do not want our confrontation with Mr King in the newspapers . . .'

'Way ahead of ye,' said Jill. 'I've put an anti-photography spell over the whole o' Glasgow Green. Don't worry, it won't affect Aunt Heather's camera, so there will be actual wedding photies. I'm also gonnae put a memory hex on all the journalists and paparazzi. Whatever happens, they'll no remember it, and they'll no get a picture of it.'

'Good,' said Ella. 'I've already told the press there's gonnae be some improvised theatre. Avant-garde, so they'll no be expecting it to make sense.'

'Clever girl,' said Jill with a warm smile.

'What aboot the polis?' said Crabbit, shifting uncomfortably under the dress she didn't feel quite herself in, and the layers of make-up that made her look almost human. 'I mean, sooner or later they'll realise they're not watching any improvised theatre.'

'I'll put a sleeping spell on them,' said Jill. 'It'll become active as soon as any magic is used. Probably when the Wee Man shows up, or King calls for his club, or Jack calls for his sword.' She sighed and rubbed the bridge of her nose. 'Boy, my Special Cupboard's gonnae be near empty by the time this is over! I hope I'm alive to care.'

'Something has been troubling me,' said Rapunzel. 'When it comes time to throw the bouquet, do we throw one each or one between the four of us?'

Jill and Ella exchanged a glance, then burst out laughing.

'What?' asked Rapunzel. 'What is funny about that?'

'I'm—I'm sorry,' Ella managed between guffaws. 'It's just . . . I wasnae expecting anyone to say anything aboot the actual wedding!'

'It's our Wedding Day,' giggled Jill. 'We cannae mention the wedding!'
The two dissolved in laughter.
The intercom buzzed and the laughter suddenly abruptly.
'Taxi's here,' said Jill.
'Aye,' replied Ella. 'This is it.'
Jill answered the intercom. 'Aye, we'll be doon in a minute.'
The four women gulped in harmony.
'Well . . . this is it,' said Jill.
'Aye,' said Ella. 'High-fives all round.'
The brides briefly slapped each other's palms, gathered their things, and
left the flat.

Jill was led down the aisle by her Fairy Godmaw; Ella by Harry's dad;
Rapunzel by the man who ran the drop-in centre where Jack did his
community service; and Crabbit by Dragonman.

The Freaks were all made up to look as normal as possible, but they
were still drawing stares and camera flashes.

Finally, the brides were lined up face-to-face with their grooms, but none
of them was able to give much thought to that. They were all distracted
by the fact that they could well be married and widowed within minutes.

'We are gathered here today,' the Minister was saying, 'to celebrate the
joining of not one couple, but four, who have chosen to join each other in
bonds of matrimony. To be cherished and loved throughout the great adventure of their lives. It is not the end of a story, mark my words . . . it is the
beginning.'

None of the brides or grooms were listening. The threat of doom was
far stronger in their bellies than the promise of joy.

Then the Minister said, 'If anyone knows of any reason why any of
these couples cannot be legally wed, let him speak now or forever hold his
peace.'

There was a great commotion as someone pushed their way through
the crowd.

The man with a wolf by his side was wearing an anorak with its hood up, mirror shades and a scarf over most of his mouth. No one who wasn't expecting him knew it was King.

All four brides and all four grooms were almost relieved to see him. This was it. It beat waiting.

'Aye!' shouted the man, as he was roundly photographed in vain. 'I know a reason yous cannae get married! You're all aboot to die!'

'Very well spoken, sir,' said the Wolf.

There was a great mutter from the crowd. They all knew to expect some sort of performance, but this was not the moment at which it had been expected.

Jack and Jill both approached King. Jill pushed her way in front of Jack.

Ella's flowing dress had a hidden compartment sewn into it, so she was able to zip the flower girl, Upenda, into the very fabric of the dress. No one noticed this taking place, as they were distracted by the outrageous behaviour of King and the Wolf.

'I'll die afore I'll let anyone touch you,' Ella whispered to her dress.

'That's no much comfort,' the dress muttered back.

Meanwhile, Jill was approaching King. 'Reggie. We've been expecting you. Hate to disappoint ye, but yer invitation didnae get lost in the post.'

'Aw, I was gonnae say that,' grumbled Jack.

'You know why I'm here,' growled King. 'Step aside.'

'Never,' said Jill. 'Only way to my family is through me.'

'I don't want to do that, Jillipoos,' said King. 'But I will, if I have to.'

'It's no too late to walk away fae this,' said Jill, softly. 'Reggie, please. Turn around and walk away. Then naebody gets hurt.'

King shook his head. 'It's gone too far for that, Jill. After what they done to me . . .'

'I didnae want them to do that. I was angry with them.'

'No angry enough to let me destroy them, though?'

'No, because whatever they done, I love them. And because . . . you did sort of bring it on yersel'.'

'Wolf,' seethed King. 'Avoid killing that one if you possibly can. Other than that . . . *kill!*'

'It would be my pleasure,' replied the Wolf. And he pounced on King.

King tried to struggle free, but the Wolf was too strong.

'Did you think you could go on fooling me?' demanded the Wolf. 'Did you think I wouldn't find out the mirror you promised to loan me was destroyed before we ever met? Oh, Mr King, it is the insult to me, as much as the deception, for which you are about to die!'

A voice from behind him cried, 'Sword!'

There was a gasp from the crowd, as a great, flaming sword appeared in Jack's hands. What power he felt as he held it high above his head! He roared as he brought it down on the wolf and cleft off the beast's head.

That might well have been the moment at which the police would have realised something very real was going on, and chosen to intervene . . . were they not fast asleep.

A flurry of flashes failed to capture the action.

The assembled guests moved back. Children screamed. Adults gasped. They were beginning to realise this was not theatre.

King rolled away, scrambled to his feet and yelled, 'Club!' The magical club of Rumpelstiltskin appeared in his hands.

For a moment, he and Jack stared at each other, wielding their respective weapons, poised to pounce.

'Shield!' cried Jack, and the magical shield was in his free hand. 'I just saved your life, mate,' he panted to King.

'Why?' demanded King.

'Because your ex-girlfriend made me promise,' said Jack. 'Go home King. We're even.'

'No we're not!' snarled King. 'You think I care about my life?' He tore off his disguise. There was a gasp as everyone present recognised him, and irrelevant cameras clicked away.

'LOOK AT ME!' cried King.

'What a pathetic creature,' spat Jill. 'I've never been happy with the way

I look, but I *live*. My life is beautiful, filled with beautiful friends. You think the looks ye had were all you had to live for? Well, maybe ye are better dead.'

There was a flash of light and Rumpelstiltskin appeared by King's side.

'Enough talking,' hissed the elf. 'Start the slaughter!'

Jack roared as he struck the creature with his flaming sword.

Rumpelstiltskin screamed and, in a great ball of fire, was gone.

In an instant, Jack had the sword back over his shoulder, poised to despatch King. 'It's over, King,' he breathed. 'Magic cannae outlive the magician. Your wee friend is dead, so your club is just a worthless hunk o' wood. You lose!'

No sooner had Jack spoken than the impotence of King's weapon was demonstrated; snatched from his hand by a lasso of Rapunzel's hair.

She pulled her pleats to safety, and Jack plunged his sword into the weapon on the ground. It was burnt to a cinder in an instant.

Rumpelstiltskin reappeared.

'You are successful,' he said, without emotion. 'You will keep your part of the bargain, I trust?'

'What?' cried King. 'I saw you die.'

'Actually, you just saw him vanish, with a wee bit o' special effects,' said Jack. 'Magic only works if ye believe it, so when you believed yer club was useless, it was.'

Jill grinned from ear to ear. 'Nicely done.'

King's eyes were wide like an animal's, as he looked this way and that in a blind panic. 'I don't understand!'

'The midget's on oor side, ya moron!' elucidated Thumbelina.

'Alas, it is true,' explained Rumpelstiltskin. 'It was I who tipped the Wolf off regarding your deception.'

'Why?'

'When I offered you alliance, it was in earnest. But circumstances have changed. I agreed to help our former enemies, and they agreed to let me spend alternate weekends with my daughter, providing I do not attempt to leave this world with her. It has been sealed with an unbreakable oath.'

'In exchange for that,' said Jack, 'we won't plaster his name all over the Internet.'

'When one says my name, its power over me diminishes but slightly. I had hoped it would soon be gone, but a million saying my name? All at once? No, I cannot cope with the magic of this modern world.' He turned his red eyes to the heavens in anguish, and made a fist.

'I had such plans for the child! I would slay her mother and her allies, and raise her as a dark elf, in a world of darkness, away from human influence, and train her well in the ways of evil!' His head dipped and he unclenched his fist. 'But I suppose there are other ways to be a good parent.'

'You have no magic mirror,' Jack told King. 'You have no magic weapon and you have no magic allies. Noo, away ye go and stop disrupting my wedding!'

King hung his head, defeated.

'Wait!' called the Frog Prince, striding forward.

'What are you doing?' demanded King. 'Get him away from me!'

The Frog Prince grabbed him firmly with his huge, black hands ... and kissed him on the forehead.

With that kiss, a yellowish glow passed over King's face ... and the scars and burns were gone. He had his old face back. He was the second-bonniest man in Glasgow again.

He screamed, holding his face. He could feel the change, but didn't know what was happening. 'What have you done to me?!' he screamed.

'Reggie, your face!' cried Jill. She borrowed a mirror from one of her bridesmaids and handed it to him.

'But why?' said King.

'It is called mercy,' said the Frog Prince. 'I give it unto thee whether thou deservest it or nay. When thou understandest why, thou wilt perhaps be a step closer to deserving.'

King felt such a flood of emotions he didn't know what to do. His reason to kill was gone, as well as his means, but the urge remained. He felt glad to have his looks back, but humiliated by the events leading up to it. He felt gratitude toward those he hated . . . but he still hated them. And he felt a new emotion, one he had never known before: humility.

It was all too much for him. He turned around and ran away, sobbing and the cheer that went up shook the very foundations of the city.

Then, when the din died down, a single voice was heard to say, 'Bob the Builder!'

The Freaks rolled on the ground laughing. Poor Crabbit got grass stains on her wedding dress.

When the laughter faded, Ella cleared her throat.

'Well,' she said. 'Noo that that wee bit o' drama's by wi', I think we should get on wi' the wedding so's we can all get down to living happily ever after.'

And that's exactly what they did.